THE
DOCTOR'S FAMILY

CHRONICLES OF CARLINGFORD

BY

MRS. OLIPHANT

First published in 1863

British Library Cataloguing-in-Publication Data
A catalogue record for this book is available
from the British Library

CONTENTS

Margaret Oliphant

Margaret Oliphant was born in Wallyford, Scotland in 1828. When she was ten years old, her family moved to Liverpool, where she began to experiment with writing. She had her first novel, *Passages in the Life of Mrs. Margaret Maitlan* (1849), published when she was just 21. It was a moderate commercial success, and following her second novel (*Caleb Field*, published in 1851) Oliphant became a regular contributor to the famous *Blackwood's Magazine*.

By the 1860s, Oliphant was a popular and recognized author, and in order to support her family (she had become a widow in 1959) she became an incredibly prolific author. Oliphant eventually went on to write more than 120 works, including novels travelogues, histories and volumes of literary criticism. Two of her better-known fictional works are *Miss Marjoribanks* (1866) and *Phoebe Junior* (1876). Towards the end of her life, she wrote a well-received series of supernatural short stories called *Tales of the Seen and Unseen* (1885), which remains popular to this day. Oliphant died in 1897, aged 69.

6

CHAPTER I.

Young Dr Rider lived in the new quarter of Carlingford: had he aimed at a reputation in society, he could not possibly have done a more foolish thing; but such was not his leading motive. The young man, being but young, aimed at a practice. He was not particular in the mean time as to the streets in which his patients dwelt. A new house, gazing with all its windows over a brick-field, was as interesting to the young surgeon as if it had been one of those exclusive houses in Grange Lane, where the aristocracy of Carlingford lived retired within their garden walls. His own establishment, though sufficiently comfortable, was of a kind utterly to shock the feelings of the refined community: a corner house, with a surgery round the corner, throwing the gleam of its red lamp over all that chaotic district of half-formed streets and full-developed brick-fields, with its night-bell prominent, and young Rider's name on a staring brass plate, with mysterious initials after it. M.R.C.S. the unhappy young man had been seduced to put after his name upon that brass plate, though he was really Dr Rider, a physician, if not an experienced one. Friends had advised him that in such districts people were afraid of physicians, associating only with dread adumbrations of a guinea a visit that miscomprehended name; so, with a pang, the young surgeon had put his degree in his pocket, and put up with the inferior distinction. Of course, Dr Marjoribanks had all the patronage of Grange Lane. The great people were infatuated about that snuffy old Scotchman—a man behind his day, who had rusted and grown old among the soft diseases of Carlingford, where sharp practice was so seldom necessary; and no opening appeared for young Rider except in the new district, in the smug corner house, with the surgery and the red lamp, and M.R.C.S.

7

on a brass plate on his door.

If you can imagine that the young man bowed his spirit to this without a struggle, you do the poor young fellow injustice. He had been hard enough put to it at divers periods of his life. Ambition had not been possible for him either in one shape or another. Some people said he had a vulgar mind when he subsided into that house; other people declared him a shabby fellow when he found out, after the hardest night's thought he ever went through in his life, that he durst not ask Bessie Christian to marry him. You don't suppose that he did not know in his secret heart, and feel tingling through every vein, those words which nobody ever said to his face? But he could not help it. He could only make an indignant gulp of his resentment and shame, which were shame and resentment at himself for wanting the courage to dare everything, as well as at other people for finding him out, and go on with his work as he best could. He was not a hero nor a martyr; men made of that stuff have large compensations. He was an ordinary individual, with no sublimity in him, and no compensation to speak of for his sufferings—no consciousness of lofty right-doing, or of a course of action superior to the world.

Perhaps you would prefer to go up-stairs and see for yourself what was the skeleton in Edward Rider's cupboard, rather than have it described to you. His drag came to the door an hour ago, and he went off with Care sitting behind him, and a certain angry pang aching in his heart, which perhaps Bessie Christian's wedding-veil, seen far off in church yesterday, might have something to do with. His looks were rather black as he twitched the reins out of his little groom's hands, and went off at a startling pace, which was almost the only consolation the young fellow had. Now that he is certainly gone, and the coast clear, we may go up-stairs. It is true he all but kicked the curate down for taking a similar liberty, but we who are less visible may venture while he is away.

This skeleton is not in a cupboard. It is in an up-stairs room, comfortable enough, but heated, close, unwholesome—a place

8

from which, even when the window is open, the fresh air seems shut out. There is no fresh air nor current of life in this stifling place. There is a fire, though it is not cold—a sofa near the fire—a sickening heavy smell of abiding tobacco—not light whiffs of smoke, such as accompany a man's labours, but a dead pall of idle heavy vapour; and in the midst of all a man stretched lazily on the sofa, with his pipe laid on the table beside him, and a book in his soft, boneless, nerveless hands. A large man, interpenetrated with smoke and idleness and a certain dreary sodden dissipation, heated yet unexcited, reading a novel he has read half-a-dozen times before. He turns his bemused eyes to the door when his invisible visitors enter. He fancies he hears some one coming, but will not take the trouble to rise and see who is there—so, instead of that exertion, he takes up his pipe, knocks the ashes out of it upon his book, fills it with coarse tobacco, and stretches his long arm over the shoulder of the sofa for a light. His feet are in slippers, his person clothed in a greasy old coat, his linen soiled and untidy. That is the skeleton in young Rider's house.

The servants, you may be sure, knew all about this unwelcome visitor. They went with bottles and jugs secretly to bring him what he wanted; they went to the circulating library for him; they let him in when he had been out in the twilight all shabby and slovenly. They would not be human if they did not talk about him. They say he is very good-natured, poor gentleman—always has a pleasant word—is nobody's enemy but his own; and to see how "the doctor do look at him, and he his own brother as was brought up with him," is dreadful, to be sure.

All this young Rider takes silently, never saying a word about it to any human creature. He seems to know by intuition what all these people say of him, as he drives about furiously in his drag from patient to patient; and wherever he goes, as plain, nay, far more distinctly than the actual prospect before him, he sees that sofa, that dusty slow-burning fire—that pipe, with the little heap of ashes knocked out of it upon the table—that wasted ruined life chafing him to desperation with its dismal content. It is very true that it would have been sadly imprudent of the young man to go to the little house in Grove Street a year ago, and tell Bessie Christian he was very fond of her, and that somehow for her love he would manage to provide for those old people whom that cheerful little woman toiled to maintain. It was a thing not to be done in any way you could contemplate it; and with a heartache the poor young doctor had turned his horse's head away from Grove Street, and left Bessie to toil on in her poverty. Bessie had escaped all that nowadays; but who could have forewarned the poor doctor that his elder brother, once the hope of the family—that clever Fred, whom all the others had been postponed to—he who with his evil reputation had driven poor Edward out of his first practice, and sent him to begin life a second time at Carlingford—was to drop listlessly in again, and lay a harder burden than a harmless old father-in-law upon the young man's hands—a burden which no grateful Bessie shared and sweetened? No wonder black Care sat at the young doctor's back as he drove at that dangerous pace through the new, encumbered streets. He might have broken his neck over those heaps of brick and mortar, and it is doubtful whether he would have greatly cared.

When Dr Rider went home that night, the first sight he saw when he pulled up at his own door was his brother's large indolent shabby figure prowling up the street. In the temper he was then in, this was not likely to soothe him. It was not a much-frequented street, but the young doctor knew instinctively that his visitor had been away in the heart of the town at the booksellers' shops buying cheap novels, and ordering them magnificently to be sent to Dr Rider's; and could guess the curious questions and large answers which had followed. He sprang to the ground with a painful suppressed indignation, intensified by many mingled feelings, and waited the arrival of the maudlin wanderer. Ah me! one might have had some consolation in the burden freely undertaken for love's sake, and by love's self shared and lightened: but this load of disgrace and ruin which nobody could take part of—which it was misery so much as to think that anybody knew of—the doctor's fraternal sentiments, blunted by absence and injury, were not strong enough to bear that weight.

"So, Fred, you have been out," said Dr Rider, moodily, as he stood aside on his own threshold to let his brother pass in—not with the courtesy of a host, but the precaution of a jailer, to see him safe before he himself entered and closed the door.

"Yes, you can't expect a man to sit in the house for ever," said the prodigal, stumbling in to his brother's favourite sitting-room, where everything was tidy and comfortable for the brief leisure of the hard-working man. The man who did no work threw himself heavily into the doctor's easy-chair, and rolled his bemused eyes round upon his brother's household gods. Those book-shelves with a bust at either corner, those red curtains drawn across the window, those prints on the walls—all once so pleasant to the doctor's eyes—took a certain air of squalor and wretchedness to-night which sickened him to look at. The lamp flared wildly with an untrimmed wick, or at least Dr Rider thought so; and threw a hideous profile of the intruder upon the wall behind him. The hearth was cold, with that chill, of sentiment rather than reality, naturally belonging to a summer night. Instead of a familiar place where rest and tranquillity awaited him, that room, the only vision of home which the poor young fellow possessed, hardened into four walls, and so many chairs and tables, in the doctor's troubled eyes.

But it bore a different aspect in the eyes of his maudlin brother. Looking round with those bewildered orbs, all this appeared luxury to the wanderer. Mentally he appraised the prints over the mantelshelf, and reckoned how much of *his*luxuries might be purchased out of them. That was all so much money wasted by the Crœsus before him. What a mint of money the fellow must be making; and grudged a little comfort to his brother, his elder brother, the cleverest of the family! The dull exasperation of selfishness woke in the mind of the self-ruined man!

"You're snug enough here," he exclaimed, "though you shut

11

me in up-stairs to burrow out of sight. By Jove! as if I were not good enough to face your Carlingford patients. I've had a better practice in my day than ever you'll see, my fine fellow, with your beggarly M.R.C.S. And you'd have me shut myself up in my garret into the bargain! You're ashamed of me, forsooth! You can go spending money on that rubbish there, and can't pay a tailor's bill for your elder brother; and as for introducing me in this wretched hole of a place, and letting me pick up a little money for myself—I, a man with twice the experience in the profession that you have——"

"Fred, stop that," cried the doctor—"I've had about enough. Look here—I can't deny you shelter and what you call necessaries, because you're my brother; but I won't submit to be ruined a second time by any man. If I am ever to do any good in this world—and whether I do any good or not," he added fiercely, "I'll not have my good name tarnished and my work interfered with *again*. I don't care two straws for my life. It's hard enough—as hard as a treadmill, and never a drop of consolation in the cup; though I might have had that if I had been anything but a fool. But look here, I do care for my practice—I won't have you put your confounded spoke in my wheel again. Keep on in your own way; smoke and drink and dream if you will; but I'll stand no interference with my work—and that I tell you once for all."

This speech was uttered with great vehemence, the speaker walking up and down the room all the while. The bitterness of ingratitude and malice had entered into the young man's soul. All the wrongs which the clever elder brother, to whose claims everybody else was subordinated, had done to his family, rose upon the recollection of the younger; all the still bitterer sting of that injury which had been personal to himself; all the burden and peril of this present undesired visit, the discontent, the threats, the evident power of doing evil, woke the temper and spirit of the young doctor. It was not Fred's fault that his brother had made that mistake in life which he repented so bitterly. Bessie Christian's bridal veil, and white ribbons; her joyful face

12

untouched with any pensive reminiscences; and the dead dulness of that house, into which foot of woman never entered, were not of Fred's doing; but passion is not reasonable. The doctor gave Fred credit unconsciously for the whole. He walked up and down the room with a whole world of passionate mortified feeling—vexation, almost despair, throbbing within him. He seemed to have made a vast sacrifice for the sake of this brother who scorned him to his face.

"You're hot," said the disreputable figure in Dr Rider's easy-chair, "much hotter than there's any occasion for. Do I envy you your beggarly patients, do you suppose? But, Ned, you never were cut out for the profession—a good shopkeeping business would have been a deal better for you. Hang it! you haven't the notions of a gentleman. You think bread and water is all you're bound to furnish your brother when he is under a cloud. As for society, I never see a soul—not even yourself, though you're no great company. Look here—I am not unreasonable; order in some supper—there's a good fellow—and let's have a comfortable evening together. You're not the man you used to be, Ned. You used to be a fellow of spirit; somebody's jilted you, or something—I don't want to pry into your secrets; but let's have a little comfort for once in a way, and you shall have the whole business about the old colony, and how I came to leave it—the truth, and nothing but the truth."

It was some time before the victim yielded; at last, half to escape the painful ferment of his own thoughts, and half with a natural yearning for some sympathy and companionship, however uncongenial, he fell out of his heat and passion into a more complacent mood. He sat down, watching with a gulp of hardly-restrained disgust that lolling figure in the chair, every gesture of which was the more distasteful for being so familiar, and recalling a hundred preliminary scenes all tending towards this total wreck and shame. Then his mind softened with fraternal instincts—strange interlacement of loathing and affection. He was tired, hungry, chilled to his heart. The spell of material comfort, even in such company, came upon the young man. They supped together, not much to the advantage of Dr Rider's head, stomach, or temper, on the following morning. The elder told his story of inevitable failure, and strange unexplainable fatality. The younger dropped forth expressions of disappointment and trouble which partly eased his own mind. Thus they spent together the unlovely evening; and perhaps a few such nights would have done as much harm to the young doctor's practice as had he introduced his disreputable brother without more ado into the particular little world of Carlingford.

CHAPTER II.

Next morning Dr Rider rose mightily vexed with himself, as was to be supposed. He was half an hour late for breakfast: he had a headache, his hand shook, and his temper was "awful." Before he was dressed, ominous knocks came to the door; and all feverish and troubled as he was, you may imagine that the prospect of the day's work before him did not improve his feelings, and that self-reproach, direst of tormentors, did not mend the matter. Two ladies were waiting for him, he was told when he went down-stairs—not to say sundry notes and messages in the ordinary way of business—two ladies who had brought two boxes with them, and asked leave to put them in the hall till they could see Dr Rider. The sight of this luggage in his little hall startled the doctor. Patients do not generally carry such things about with them. What did it mean? What could two ladies want with him? The young man felt his face burn with painful anticipations, a little shame, and much impatience. Probably the sister who adored Fred, and never could learn to believe that he was not unfortunate and a victim. This would be a climax to the occupation of his house.

As the poor doctor gloomily approached the door of the room in which he had spent last evening, he heard a little rustle and commotion not quite consistent with his expectations—a hum of voices and soft stir such as youthful womankind only makes. Then a voice entirely strange to him uttered an exclamation. Involuntarily he started and changed his aspect. He did not know the voice, but it was young, sweet, peculiar. The cloud lightened a little upon the doctor's face. Notwithstanding Bessie Christian, he was still young enough to feel a little flutter of curiosity when he heard such a voice sounding out of his room. Hark! what did she say? It was a profoundly prosaic speech.

"What an intolerable smell of smoke! I shouldn't wonder a bit—indeed, I rather think he must be, or he wouldn't live in a place like this—if he were exactly such another as Fred."

"Poor Fred!" said a plaintive voice, "if we only can learn where he is. Hush, there is a footstep! Ah, it is not my poor fellow's footstep! Nettie, hark!"

"No, indeed! twenty thousand times sharper, and more like a man," said the other, in hurried breathless accents. "Hark! here he is."

The entire bewilderment, the amaze, apprehension, confusion with which Dr Rider entered the room from which this scrap of conversation reached him, is indescribable. A dreadful sense that something was about to happen seized the young man's mind with an indescribable curiosity. He paused an instant to recover himself, and then went boldly and silently into the room which had become mysterious through its new inmates. They both turned round upon him as he entered. Two young women: one who had been sitting at the table, looking faded, plaintive, and anxious, rose up suddenly, and, clasping her hands, as if in entreaty, fixed two bright but sunken eyes upon his face. The other, a younger, lighter figure, all action and haste, interposed between him and her companion. She put up one hand in warning to the petitioner behind her, and one to call the attention of the bewildered stranger before. Evidently the one thing which alarmed this young lady was that somebody would speak before her, and the conduct of the *situation* be taken out of her hands. She was little, very slight, very pretty, but her prettiness was peculiar. The young doctor, accustomed to the fair Saxon version of beauty given by Bessie Christian, did not at the first glance believe that the wonderful little person before him possessed any; for she was not only slender, but *thin*, dark, eager, impetuous, with blazing black eyes and red lips, and nothing else notable about her. So he thought, gazing fascinated, yet not altogether attracted—scarcely sure that he was not repelled—

16

unable, however, to withdraw his eyes from that hurried, eager little figure. Nothing in the least like her had ever yet appeared before Dr Rider's eyes.

"We want to inquire about your brother," said the little stranger; "we know this was to be his address, and we want to know whether he is living here. His letters were to be sent to your care; but my sister has not heard from him now for a year."

"Never mind that!—never mind telling that, Nettie," cried the other behind her. "Oh, sir! only tell me where my poor Fred is?"

"So she began to fear he was ill," resumed the younger of the two, undauntedly; "though Susan will do nothing but praise him, he has behaved to her very shamefully. Do you happen to know, sir, where he is?"

"Did you say Fred—my brother Fred?" cried the poor young doctor in utter dismay; "and may I ask who it is that expresses so much interest in him?"

There was a momentary pause; the two women exchanged looks. "I told you so," cried the eager little spokeswoman. "He never has let his friends know; he was afraid of that. I told you how it was. This," she continued, with a little tragic air, stretching out her arm to her sister, and facing the doctor—"this is Mrs Frederick Rider, or rather Mrs Rider, I should say, as he is the eldest of the family! Now will you please to tell us where he is?"

The doctor made no immediate answer. He gazed past the speaker to the faded woman behind, and exclaimed, with a kind of groan, "Fred's wife!"

"Yes, Fred's wife," cried the poor creature, rushing forward to him; "and oh! where is he? I've come thousands of miles to hear. Is he ill? has anything happened to him? Where is Fred?"

"Susan, you are not able to manage this; leave it to me," said her sister, drawing her back peremptorily. "Dr Rider, please to answer us. We know you well enough, though you don't seem ever to have heard of us. It was you that my brother-in-law gave up his business to before he came out to the colony. Oh, we know all about it! To keep him separate from his wife cannot do you any benefit, Dr Edward. Yes, I know your name, and all about it; and I don't mean indeed to suffer my sister to be injured and kept from her husband. I have come all this way with her to take care of her. I mean to stay with her to take care of her. I have not parted with my money, though she gave all hers away; and I mean to see her have her rights."

"Oh, Nettie, Nettie, how you talk!" cried the unfortunate wife. "You keep him from answering me. All this time I cannot hear—where is Fred?"

"Be seated, please," said the doctor, with dreadful civility, "and compose yourselves. Fred is well enough; as well as he ever is. I don't know," added poor Rider, with irrestrainable bitterness, "whether he is quite presentable to ladies; but I presume, madam, if you're his wife, you're acquainted with his habits. Excuse me for being quite unprepared for such a visit. I have not much leisure for anything out of my profession. I can scarcely spare these minutes, that is the truth; but if you will favour me with a few particulars, I will have the news conveyed to my brother. I—I beg your pardon. When a man finds he has new relations he never dreamed of, it naturally embarrasses him at the moment. May I ask if you ladies have come from Australia alone?"

"Oh, not alone; the children are at the hotel. Nettie said it was no use coming unless we all came," said his new sister-in-law, with a half-sob.

"The children!" Dr Rider's gasp of dismay was silent, and made no sound. He stood staring blankly at those wonderful invaders of his bachelor house, marvelling what was to be done with them in the first place. Was he to bring Fred down all slovenly and half-awakened? was he to leave them in possession of his private sanctuary? The precious morning moments were passing while he pondered, and his little groom fidgeted outside with a message for the doctor. While he stood irresolute, the indefatigable Nettie once more darted forward.

"Give me Fred's address, please," said this managing woman. "I'll see him, and prepare him for meeting Susan. He can say what he pleases to me; *I* don't mind it in the very least; but Susan of course must be taken care of. Now, look here, Dr Edward; Susan is your sister-in-law, and I am her sister. We don't want to occupy your time. I can manage everything; but it is quite necessary in the first place that you should confide in me."

"Confide!" cried the bewildered man. "Fred is not under my authority. He is here in my house much against my will. He is in bed, and not fit to be awakened; and I am obliged to tell you simply, ladies," said the unfortunate doctor, "that my house has no accommodation for a family. If you will go back to the hotel where you left the children"—and here the speaker gave another gasp of horror—"I'll have him roused and sent to you. It is the only thing I can do."

"Susan can go," said the prompt Nettie; "I'll stay here until Fred is ready, and take him to see them. It is necessary he should be prepared, you know. Don't talk nonsense, Susan—I shall stay here, and Dr Rider, of course, will call a cab for you."

"But Nettie, Nettie dear, it isn't proper. I can't leave you all by yourself in a strange house," remonstrated her sister.

"Don't talk such stuff; I am perfectly well able to take care of myself; I am not a London young lady," said the courageous Nettie. "It is perfectly unnecessary to say another word to me—I know my duty—I shall stay here."

With which speech she seated herself resolutely in that same easy-chair which Fred had lolled in last night, took off her bonnet, for hats were not in these days, and shed off from her face, with two tiny hands, exquisite in shape if a little brown in colour, the great braids of dark-brown silky hair which encumbered her little head. The gesture mollified Dr Rider in the most unaccountable way in spite of himself. The intolerable idea of leaving these two in his house became less intolerable, he could not tell how. And the little groom outside fairly knocked at the door in that softening moment with a message which could be delayed no longer. The doctor put his head out to receive the call, and looked in again perplexed and uncertain. Nettie had

19

quite established herself in the easy-chair. She sat there looking with her bright eyes into the vacant air before her, in a pretty attitude of determination and readiness, beating her little foot on the carpet. Something whimsical, odd, and embarrassing about her position made it all the more piquant to the troubled eyes which, in spite of all their worldly wisdom, were still the eyes of a young man. He could not tell in the world what to say to her. To order that creature out of his house was simply impossible; to remain there was equally so; to leave them in possession of the field—what could the unfortunate young doctor do? One thing was certain, the impatient patient could no longer be neglected; and after a few minutes longer of bewildered uncertainty, Dr Rider went off in the wildest confusion of mind, leaving his brother's unknown family triumphant in his invaded house.

To describe the feelings with which the unfortunate doctor went fasting about his day's work—the manner in which that scene returned to him after every visit he made—the continual succession in which wrath, dismay, alarm, bitter disgust with the falsehood of the brother who, no further gone than last night, had pretended to confide in him, but never breathed a syllable of this biggest unconcealable secret, swept through the mind of the victim; all culminating, however, in the softening of that moment, in the tiny figure, indomitable elf or fairy, shedding back with dainty fingers those soft abundant locks—would be impossible. The young man got through his work somehow, in a maze of confusion and excitement—angry excitement, indignant confusion, determination to yield nothing further, but to defend himself and his house once for all from the inroads of what he angrily pronounced in his own mind "another man's family"— yet, withal, of curiosity and interest which gave zest greater than usual to the idea of going home. When he was able at last to turn his horse's head towards his own dwelling, it was with feelings very different from the usual unexpecting blank of sullen displeasure. What he should find there, was a curious, exciting, alarming question; perhaps an entire nursery with Nettie in

20

charge; perhaps a recusant husband with Nettie mounting guard over him; perhaps a thrilling scene of family explanation and reconciliation. The day had been a specially long and hard one. He had been obliged to snatch a hurried lunch at one of his patients' houses, and to postpone his hard-earned dinner to the most fashionable of hours. It was indeed quite evening, almost twilight, when he made his way home at last. As he neared the scene of action, the tired man condoled with himself over the untimely excitement that awaited him. He said to himself with pathetic self-pity that it was hard indeed for a man who had earned a little repose to go in upon all the troubles of another man's family. He had denied himself—he had not undertaken upon his own shoulders that pleasing burden; and now what was he to be saddled with?—the burden without the consolation—the responsibility without the companionship. All this Dr Rider represented to himself very pathetically as he wended his homeward way. Yet it is astonishing, notwithstanding, with what alacrity he hastened upon that path, and how much the curiosity, the excitement, the dramatic stir and commotion made in his monotonous life by this entirely new unexpected incident, occupied his mind. With expectations highly roused, he drew up once more before his own house. It was surprising to him to see how exactly it looked like itself. The blinds half-drawn down in the genteelest calm as they always were—no faces peeping at the windows—no marks of an arrival on the pavement, or in the composed countenance of Mary, who stood holding the door open for him. He went in with a little thrill of curiosity; the house was very quiet—dead-quiet in comparison with the commotion of his thoughts; so was the sitting-room where he had left Nettie resolutely planted in the easy-chair; there was nobody there now; the boxes were out of the hall, not a sound was to be heard in the house. He turned rather blankly upon Mary, who was going away quite composedly, as if there was nothing which she wanted to tell or he to hear.

"Where is my brother and the ladies?" said the amazed doctor.

"They all went off to the 'otel, sir, as soon as Mr Rider came down-stairs," said Mary, complacently. "I assured Miss as it was the best thing she could do, sir, for that I was 'most sure you'd never have the children here,—as to be sure there wasn't no room neither," said the doctor's factotum. "As soon as Mr Frederick came down, she called a cab, did Miss, and took 'em both away."

"Oh! so they're gone, are they?" said the doctor.

"Hours and hours ago," answered Mary; "dinner 'll be up in two minutes. But I wouldn't say much for the potatoes, sir. When a gentleman's irreg'lar, it's hard laws on the poor servants—nothink will keep, going on for two hours, and not take no harm; but all's quiet and comfortable in your room."

And with this assurance, which she evidently thought a very grateful one, Mary went off to get the doctor's dinner. He walked to the end of the room, and then back again, with solemnity—then threw himself into that easy-chair. "Blessed riddance!" said the doctor; but somehow he looked glum, wonderfully glum. There was no accounting for those blank looks of his; he who had been condoling with himself over the exciting scene he expected, so uncomfortable a conclusion to a long day's labour, how was it he did not look relieved when that scene was spared him? To tell the truth, when one has been expecting something to happen, of whatever description, and has been preparing one's courage, one's temper, one's fortitude, in anticipatory rehearsals—when one has placed one's self in the attitude of a martyr, and prepared to meet with fiery trials—it is mortifying, to say the least, when one finds all the necessities of the case disappear, and the mildest calm replace that tragical anticipation: the quiet falls blank upon the excited fancy. Of course Dr Rider was relieved; but it was with something mightily like disappointment that he leant back in his chair and knitted his brows at the opposite wall. Not for the world would he have acknowledged himself to be disappointed; but the calm was wonderfully monotonous after all those expectations. He was never so bored and sick of a night by himself. He tried to read, but reading did not occupy his mind. He grew furious over his charred chops and sodden potatoes. As for the tea Mary brought, he would have gladly pitched it at her by way of diversifying that blank evening with an incident. The contrast between what he had looked for and what he had, was wonderful. How delicious this stillness should have been, this consciousness of having his house to himself, and nobody to interrupt his brief repose! But somehow it appears that human nature takes best with not having its wishes granted. It is indescribable how Dr Rider yawned—how dull he found his newspaper—how few books worth reading there were in the house—how slow the minutes ran on. If somebody had chosen to be ill that night, of all nights the best for such a purpose, the doctor would not have objected to such an interruption. Failing that, he went to bed early, dreadfully tired of his own society. Such were the wonderful results of that invasion so much dreaded, and that retreat so much hoped for. Perhaps his own society had never in his life been so distasteful to him before.

CHAPTER III.

Next day Dr Rider audibly congratulated himself at breakfast upon having once more his house to himself—audibly, as if it were really necessary to give utterance to the thought before he could quite feel its force. A week before, if Fred had departed, however summarily, there can be no doubt that his brother's feelings of relief and comfort would have been unfeigned; now, however, he began to think the matter over, and to justify to himself his extraordinary sense of disappointment. As he poured out his own coffee with a sober face, his eye rested upon that easy-chair which had been brought into such prominence in the history of the last two days. He kept looking at it as he sipped that gloomy coffee. Fred had faded from the great chair; his big image threw no shadow upon it. There sat a little fairy queen, tiny as Titania, but dark as an elf of the East, putting up those two shapely tiny hands, brown and beautiful, to push aside the flood of hair, which certainly would have veiled her little figure all over, the doctor thought, had it been let down. Wonderful little sprite! She, no doubt, had dragged her plaintive sister over the seas— she it was that had forced her way into Edward Rider's house; taken her position in it, ousted the doctor; and she doubtless it was who swept the husband and wife out of it again, leaving no trace behind. Waking up from a little trance of musing upon this too interesting subject, Dr Rider suddenly raised himself into an erect position, body and mind, with an involuntary movement, as if to shake off the yoke of the enchantress. He reminded himself instinctively of his brother's falsehood and ingratitude. After throwing himself a most distasteful burden on Edward's charity for five long dreary months, the bugbear of the doctor's dreams, and heavy ever-recurring climax of his uncomfortable thoughts, here had Fred departed without a word of explanation or thanks, or even without saying good-bye. The doctor thought himself quite justified in being angry. He began to feel that the suspicious uneasiness which possessed him was equally natural and inevitable. Such a thankless, heartless departure was enough to put any man out. To imagine that Fred could be capable of it, naturally went to his brother's heart.

That day there was still no word of the party who had disappeared so mysteriously out of the doctor's house. Dr Rider went to his hard day's work vaguely expectant, feeling sure he must hear of them somehow, and more interested in hearing of them than was to be expected from his former low ebb of fraternal affection. When he returned and found still no letter, no message, the blank disappointment of the former night closed still more blankly upon him. When one is all by one's self, and has nothing at best but an easy-chair to go home to, and goes home expecting a letter, or a message, or a visitor who has not arrived, and has no chance of arriving, the revulsion of feeling is not agreeable. It did not improve the doctor's temper in the first place. The chill loneliness of that trim room, with its drawn curtains and tidy pretence of being comfortable, exasperated him beyond bearing. He felt shut up in it, and yet would not leave it. Somebody certainly might come even to-night. Fred himself perhaps, if he could escape from the rigid guardianship he was under; or was that miraculous Australian Nettie a little witch, who had spirited the whole party in a nutshell over the seas? Never was man delivered from a burden with a worse grace than was Dr Rider; and the matter had not mended in these twenty-four hours.

Next morning, however, this fever of fraternal suspense was assuaged. A three-cornered note, addressed in an odd feminine hand, very thin, small, and rapid, came among Dr Rider's letters. He signalled it out by instinct, and opened it with an impatience wonderful to behold.

"Sir,—We are all at the Blue Boar until we can get lodgings, which I hope to be to-day. I am utterly ashamed of Fred for not having let you know, and indeed of myself for trusting to him. I should not wonder but we may have been under a mistake about him and you. If you could call about one, I should most likely be in to see you, and perhaps you could give me your advice about the lodgings. Neither of *them* have the least judgment in such matters. I am sorry to trouble you; but being a stranger, perhaps you will excuse me. I understand you are only at home in the evening, and that is just the time I can't come out, as I have the whole of them to look to, which is the reason I ask you to call on me. Begging you will pardon me, I remain,

"Nettie Underwood."

"She remains Nettie Underwood," said the doctor, unawares. He laughed to himself at that conclusion. Then an odd gleam came across his face. It was probably the first time he had laughed in a natural fashion for some months back, and the unusual exertion made his cheeks tingle. His temper was improved that morning. He went off to his patients almost in a good humour. When he passed the great house where Bessie Christian now reigned, he recalled her image with a positive effort. Astonishing what an effect of distance had floated over the apparition of that bride. Was it a year since he saw her and gnashed his teeth at the thought of his own folly, or was it only last Sunday? The doctor could not tell. He put Nettie's note in his pocket-book, and was at the hotel door punctually at one o'clock. It was in the principal street of Carlingford, George Street, where all the best shops, and indeed some of the best houses, were. From the corner window of the hotel you could see down into the bowery seclusion of Grange Lane, and Mr Wodehouse's famous apple-trees holding tempting clusters over the high wall. The prospect was very different from that which extended before Dr Rider's window. Instinctively he marvelled within himself whether, if Dr Marjoribanks were to die—people cannot live for ever even in Carlingford—whether it might not be a disadvantage to a man to live so far out of the world. No doubt it was a temptation of the Evil One. Happily the young man did not take sufficient time to answer himself, but walked forward briskly through the mazy old passages of the old inn, to a room from which sundry noises issued. Dr Rider walked in with the natural confidence of a man who has an appointment. The room was in undisturbed possession of three children—three children making noise enough for six—all very small, very precocious, with staring round eyes and the most complete independence of speech and manners. The doctor confronted the little rabble thunderstruck; they were his brother's children, unrecognisable little savages as they were. One little fellow, in a linen pinafore, was mounted on the arm of a sofa, spurring vigorously; another was pursuing his sister about the room, trying to catch her feet with the tongs, and filling the air with repeated loud snaps of disappointment. They intermitted their occupations to stare at him. "Look here—here's a man," said the youngest, meditatively, beholding his dismayed uncle with a philosophic eye. "Can't some one go and tell Nettie?" said the little girl, gazing also with calm equanimity. "If he wants Nettie he'll have to wait," said the elder boy. A pause followed; the unhappy doctor stood transfixed by the steady stare of their three pair of eyes. Suddenly the little girl burst out of the room, and ran screaming along the passage. "Mamma, mamma, here's a man come," cried the wonderful colonial child. A few minutes afterwards their mother appeared, languid and faded as before. Perhaps she had been even prettier than Nettie in her bright days, if any days had ever been bright for Fred Rider's wife. She was fairer, larger, smoother than her sister; but these advantages had lapsed in a general fade, which transformed her colour into washy pinkness, made her figure stoop, and her footsteps drag. She came remonstrating all the way in feeble accents. It was not for her, certainly, that the doctor had taken the trouble to come to the Blue Boar.

"Please to sit down," said Mrs Fred, and stood leaning on the table, looking at her brother-in-law with a calm curiosity, not unlike that of her children. "Nettie and my husband have gone out together; but now that we are all so happy and united," she continued, with a sort of feeble spitefulness, "I am sure it is quite a pity to trouble you. You could not take us in, you know. You said that very plain, Mr Edward."

"It was perfectly true, madam," said the doctor. "I have not ventured on the step my brother has taken, and have naturally no accommodation for a family. But I am not here for my own pleasure. Your sister, I presume it is, wrote to me. I was requested to call here to-day."

"Oh, yes; Nettie is very self-willed—very; though, of course, we could not get on without her. She attacked Fred like a wild-cat for not writing you: but I daresay, if the truth were known, you did not expect to hear from my husband," said the wife, recovering her voice, and fixing a vindictive gaze upon her visitor, who felt himself betrayed.

"I came by Miss Underwood's instructions and at her request," said the unfortunate man. "We need not enter into any question between Fred and myself."

"Ah, yes, that is very safe and wise for you," laughed Fred's wife.

The doctor was deeply exasperated, as was only natural: he eyed the feeble helpless creature for a moment angrily, provoked to answer her; but his gaze became one of wonder and dismay ere he withdrew it. Surely of all incomprehensible entities, the most amazing is a fool—a creature insensate, unreasoning, whom neither argument nor fact can make any impression upon. Appalled and impressed, the doctor's gaze left that pretty faded face to turn upon the children. Dreadful imps! If Fred had only taken to evil ways after he became possessed of such a family, his brother could have forgiven him. While these thoughts passed through Dr Rider's mind, however, deliverance approached. He heard Nettie's voice in the passage, long before she reached the door. Not that it was loud like the voices of this dreadful household; but the tone was sufficiently peculiar to be recognised anywhere. With a most penetrating clearness, it came through the long passages, words inaudible, only the sound of a voice, rapid, breathless, decided—with the distant sound of Fred's long, shambling, uncertain footsteps coming in as the strange accompaniment. Then they entered the room— the one tiny, bright, dauntless, an intrepid, undiscourageable little soul; the other with his heavy large limbs, his bemused face, his air of hopeless failure, idleness, content. Edward Rider gazed involuntarily from one to another of this two. He saw the sprite place herself between the husband and wife, a vain little Quixote, balancing these extremes of helplessness and ruin. He could not help looking at her with a certain unconscious admiration and amazement, as he might have looked at a forlorn hope. Thousands of miles away from her friends, wherever and whatever they might be, with Fred and his wife and children on her hands, a household of incapables—what was that little creature to do?

"Good morning, Dr Edward," said Nettie. "I thought I should have been back sooner; but Fred is so slow, I cannot manage to get him along at all. We have found some lodgings a little way out of Carlingford, near that chapel, you know, or church, or something, that stands a little off the road: where it's open, and there's morning service, and such a handsome young clergyman. Who is he? We went into the chapel, and it's so fine, you would not believe it. Well, just a hundred yards from there is the house. Four rooms, exactly what I wanted, with a garden for the children to play in—quite quiet, and fresh and pleasant. Tell me who the people are—their name is Smith. If they're respectable, I'll go back and take it. I can afford the rent."

"Near St Roque's? They belong to the church there. I daresay they are all right," said the doctor, "but it is a long way off, and inconvenient, and——"

"That is just why I want it," said Nettie. "We never were used to conveniences, and none of us want to be much in the town, so far as I know. It is the very thing. Why has not lunch come up?—what do these people mean, Susan, by not attending to their orders? Ring the bell, Freddy—ring loud; and after lunch, as your drag is at the door, Dr Edward, you'll drive me down to this place again, that I may secure it, won't you? I want to have a talk with you besides.—Lunch, please, immediately. I ordered it to be ready at one—now it is half-past. We can't have our time wasted this way.—Dr Edward, please, you'll stay."

The doctor gazed with ever-increasing amazement at the little speaker. Nobody else had spoken a word. Fred had nodded to him sullenly. Fred's wife had sunk back on the sofa—everybody seemed to recognise Nettie as supreme. He hesitated, it must be confessed, to put his grievances so entirely aside as to sit down in perfect amity with Fred and his household; but to refuse to drive Nettie to St Roque's was impossible. The blood rushed to the doctor's face at the thought. What the world of Carlingford would say to see his well-known vehicle proceeding down Grange Lane, through Dr Marjoribanks's territories, under such circumstances, was a question he did not choose to consider; neither did he enter too minutely into the special moment at which his next patient might be expecting him. The young man was under the spell, and did not struggle against it. He yielded to the invitation, which was a command. He drew near the table at which Nettie, without hesitation, took the presiding place. A dull amount of conversation, often interrupted by that lively little woman, rose in the uncongenial party. Nettie cut up the meat for those staring imps of children—did them all up in snowy napkins—kept them silent and in order. She regulated what Susan was to have, and which things were best for Fred. She appealed to Dr Edward perpetually, taking him into her confidence in a way which could not fail to be flattering to that young man, and actually reduced to the calmness of an ordinary friendly party this circle so full of smouldering elements of commotion. Through all she was so dainty, so pretty, her rapid fingers so shapely, her eager talk so sweet-toned, that it was beyond the power of mortal man to remain uninterested. It was a development of womankind unknown to Dr Rider. Bessie

Christian had exhausted the race for him until now; but Nettie was a thousand times more piquant than Bessie Christian. He gazed and wondered, and moralised secretly in his own mind, what was to become of the girl?—what could she do?

"You have left some of your things at my house, Fred," said the doctor, making an attempt to approach his sullen brother, who evidently expected no overtures of friendship.

"Yes. Mrs Rider, you see, arrived unexpectedly," said Fred, with confusion—"in fact, I knew nothing about it, or—or I should have told you—Nettie——"

"Nettie thought it best to come off at once, without writing," explained Fred's wife.

"What was the use of writing?" cried that little person. "You had written to Fred for six months without ever getting an answer. You made everybody unhappy round you with your fears and troubles about him. I knew perfectly he was quite well and enjoying himself; but, of course, Susan would not be convinced. So what was there for it but bringing her away? What else could I do, Dr Edward? And to leave the children would have been preposterous. In the first place, I should have been miserable about them; and so, as soon as she found Fred was all right, would Susan: and something would certainly have happened—scarlet fever or something—and at the end of all I should have had to go out again to fetch them. So the shortest way was to bring them at once. Don't you think so? And to see us all here so comfortable, I am sure is enough to repay any one for the trouble. Fred, don't drink any more beer."

Nettie put out her tiny hand as she spoke to arrest the bottle. Fred stared at her with a dull red flush on his face; but he gave in, in the most inexplicable way; it seemed a matter of course to yield to Nettie. The doctor's amazement began to be mingled with amusement. To see how she managed them all was worth the sacrifice of a little time—unconsciously he became more fraternal in his thoughts. He spoke to foolish faded Mrs Fred with a total forgiveness and forgetfulness of her spiteful speech.

He hoped she would like Carlingford; he said something to the children. But it was not easy to talk in presence of that amazing family party, the existence of which he had not dreamed of a few days ago. To see his brother at the head of such a group had, in spite of himself, a wonderful effect upon Dr Rider. Their children, of course, must be supported somehow. Who was to do it? Was their father, grown incapable and useless in the middle of his days, to be forced into the current of life again? Was it a vague faith in Providence which had brought the helpless household here; or was it a more distinct, if not so elevated, confidence in Nettie? The doctor's heart sank once more within him as he looked round the table. Three helpless by nature—two equally helpless who ought in nature to have been the support of the whole—nothing but one bright ready little spirit between them all and destitution; and what could Nettie do to stave that wolf from the door? Once more Dr Rider's countenance fell. If the household broke down in its attempt at independence, who had they to turn to but himself?—such a prospect was not comfortable. When a man works himself to death for his own family, he takes the pleasure with the pain; but when another's family threatens to fall upon his hands, the prospect is naturally appalling—and even if Fred could do anything, what was Fred's life, undermined by evil habit, to depend upon? Silence once more fell over the little company—silence from all but Nettie and the children, who referred to her naturally instead of to their mother. Fred was sullen, and his wife took her cue from him. Edward was uneasy and dismayed. Family parties suddenly assembled without due warning are seldom greatly successful; and even Nettie could not make immediate reconciliation and fraternal kindness out of this.

CHAPTER IV.

"Take me down this long pretty road. There must be delicious houses inside the walls. Look here; drive slowly, and let us have a peep in at this open door," said Nettie. "How sweet and cosy! and who is that pretty young lady coming out? I saw her in the chapel this morning. Oh," added Nettie, with a little sharpness, "she knows *you*—tell me who she is."

"That is Miss Lucy Wodehouse—one of our Carlingford beauties," said Dr Rider.

"Do you know her very well?" asked the inquisitive Nettie. "How she stares—why does she stare, do you suppose? Is there anything absurd about my dress? Look here—don't they wear bonnets just like this in England?"

"So far as I am able to judge," said the doctor, looking at the tiny head overladen with hair, from which the bonnet had fallen half off.

"I suppose she is surprised to see me here. Drive on faster, Dr Edward, I want to talk to you. I see Fred has been telling us a parcel of stories. It would be cruel to tell Susan, you know, for she believes in him; but you may quite trust me. Is your brother good for anything, Dr Edward, do you suppose?"

"Not very much now, I fear," said the doctor.

"Not very much *now*. I suppose he never was good for much," said the indignant Nettie; "but he was said to be very clever when he first came out to the colony. I can't tell why Susan married him. She is very self-willed, though you would fancy her so submissive. She is one of those people, you know, who fall ill when they are crossed, and threaten to die, so that one daren't cross her. Now, then, what is to be done with them? He will not go back to the colony, and I don't care to do it myself. Must I keep

33

them here?"

"Miss Underwood——" began the perplexed doctor.

"It would save trouble to call me Nettie—everybody does," said his strange companion; "besides, you are my brother in a kind of a way, and the only person I can consult with; for, of course, it would not do to tell one's difficulties to strangers. Fred may not be very much to depend upon, you know, but still he is Fred."

"Yes," said the doctor, with a little self-reproach, "still he is Fred; but pardon me, the name suggests long aggravations. You can't tell how often I have had to put up with affronts and injuries because it was Fred. I shouldn't like to grieve you——"

"Never mind about grieving me;—*I* am not in love with him;—let me hear all about it!" said Nettie.

Dr Rider paused a little; seeing the abyss upon the brink of which this brave little girl was standing, he had not the heart to aggravate her by telling the failures of the past. Better to soften the inevitable discovery if possible. But his hesitation was quite apparent to Nettie. With considerable impatience she turned round upon him.

"If you think I don't know what I am doing, but have gone into this business like a fool, you are quite mistaken, Dr Edward," she said, a little sharply. "I see how it is as well as anybody can do. I knew how it was when I left the colony. Don't be alarmed about me. Do you think I am to be turned against my own flesh and blood by finding out their follies; or to grumble at the place God put me in?—Nothing of the sort! I know the kind of situation perfectly—but one *may* make the best of it, you know: and for that reason tell me everything, please."

"But, Miss Underwood, consider," cried the doctor, in consternation. "You are taking responsibilities upon yourself which nobody could lay upon you; you! young—tender" (the doctor paused for a word, afraid to be too complimentary)— "delicate! Why, the whole burden of this family will come upon you. There is not one able to help himself in the whole bundle! I

am shocked!—I am alarmed!—I don't know what to say to you—
—"

"Don't say anything, please," said Nettie. "I know what I am
about. Do you call this a street or a lane, or what do you call it?
Oh, such nice houses! shouldn't I like to be able to afford to have
one of them, and nurses, and governesses, and everything proper
for the children! I should like to dress them so nicely, and give
them such a good education. I don't know anything particular
to speak of, myself—I shall never be able to teach them when
they grow older. If Fred, now, was only to be trusted, and would
go and work like a man and make something for the children, I
daresay I could keep up the house;—but if he won't do anything,
you know, it will take us every farthing just to live. Look here,
Dr Edward: I have two hundred a-year;—Susan had the same,
you know, but Fred got all the money when they were married,
and muddled it away. Now, how much can one do in Carlingford
with three children upon two hundred a-year?"

"Fred will be the meanest blackguard in existence," cried the
doctor, "if he takes his living from you."

"He took his living from _you_, it appears," said Nettie, coolly,
"and did not thank you much. We must make the best of him.
We can't help ourselves. Now, there is the pretty church, and
there is our little house. Come in with me and answer for me,
Dr Edward. You can say I am your sister-in-law, you know, and
then, perhaps, we can get into possession at once; for," said Nettie,
suddenly turning round upon the doctor with her brilliant eyes
shining out quaintly under the little brow all puckered into
curves of foresight, "it is so sadly expensive living where we are
now."

To look at the creature thus flashing those shining eyes, not
without a smile lurking in their depths, upon him—to see the
triumphant, undaunted, undoubting youthfulness which never
dreamt of failure—to note that pretty anxiety, the look which
might have become a bride in her first troubles "playing at
housekeeping," and think how desperate was the position she had

assumed, how dreary the burden she had taken upon her—was almost too much for the doctor's self-control. He did not know whether to admire the little heroine as half-divine, or to turn from her as half-crazy. Probably, had the strange little spirit possessed a different frame, the latter was the sentiment which would have influenced the unimaginative mind of Edward Rider. But there was no resisting that little brown Titania, with her little head overladen with its beautiful hair, her red, delicate mouth closing firm and sweet above that little decided chin, her eyes which seemed to concentrate the light. She seemed only a featherweight when the bewildered doctor helped her to alight—an undoubted sprite and creature of romance. But to hear her arranging about all the domestic necessities within, and disclosing her future plans for the children, and all the order of that life of which she took the charge so unhesitatingly, bewildered the mistress of the house as much as it did the wondering doctor. The two together stood gazing at her as she moved about the room, pouring forth floods of eager talk. Her words were almost as rapid as her step,—her foot, light as it was, almost as decided and firm as her resolutions. She was a wonder to behold as she pushed about the furniture, and considered how it could be brightened up and made more comfortable. Gazing at her with his silent lips apart, Dr Rider sighed at the word. Comfortable! Was she to give her mind to making Fred and his children comfortable— such a creature as this? Involuntarily it occurred to Edward that, under such ministrations, sundry changes might come over the aspect of that prim apartment in which he had seen her first; the room with the bookcase and the red curtains, and the prints over the mantelpiece—a very tidy, comfortable room before any bewitching imp came to haunt it, and whisper suspicions of its imperfection—the doctor's own retirement, where he had chewed the cud of sweet and bitter fancies often enough, without much thought of his surroundings. But Nettie now had taken possession of the prosaic place, and, all unconscious of that spiritual occupation, was as busy and as excited about Mrs

Smith's lodgings at St Roque's Cottage as if it were an ideal home she was preparing, and the life to be lived in it was the brightest and most hopeful in the world.

When Dr Rider reached home that night, and took his lonely meal in his lonely room, certain bitter thoughts of unequal fortune occupied the young man's mind. Let a fellow be but useless, thankless, and heartless enough, and people spring up on all sides to do his work for him, said the doctor to himself, with a bitterness as natural as it was untrue. The more worthless a fellow is, the more all the women connected with him cling to him and make excuses for him, said Edward Rider in his indignant heart. Mother and sister in the past—wife and Nettie now—to think how Fred had secured for himself such perpetual ministrations, by neglecting all the duties of life! No wonder an indignant pang transfixed the lonely bosom of the virtuous doctor, solitary and unconsoled as he was. *His* laborious days knew no such solace. And as he fretted and pondered, no visions of Bessie Christian perplexed his thoughts. He had forgotten that young woman. All his mind was fully occupied chafing at the sacrifice of Nettie. He was not sorry, he was angry, to think of her odd position, and the duties she had taken upon herself. What had she to do with those wretched children, and that faded spiteful mother? Edward Rider was supremely disgusted. He said to himself, with the highest moral indignation, that such a girl ought not to be permitted to tie herself to such a fate.

CHAPTER V.

St Roque's Cottage was considered rather a triumph of local architecture. A Carlingford artist had built it "after" the Church, which was one of Gilbert Scott's churches, and perfect in its way, so that its Gothic qualities were unquestionable. The only thing wanting was size, which was certainly an unfortunate defect, and made this adaptation of ecclesiastical architecture to domestic purposes a very doubtful experiment. However, in bright sunshine, when the abundance of light neutralised the want of window, all was well, and there was still abundance of sunshine in Carlingford in October, three months after the entrance of Fred Rider and his family into Mrs Smith's little rooms. It was a bright autumn day, still mild, though with a crispness in the air, the late season showing more in the destitution of the flower-borders than in any more sensible sign. It was a pretty spot enough for a roadside. St Roque's stood on the edge of a little common, over which, at the other margin, you could see some white cottages, natural to the soil, in a little hamlet-cluster, dropped along the edge of the grey-green unequal grass; while between the church and the cottage ran the merest shadow of a brook, just enough to give place and nutriment to three willow-trees which had been the feature of the scene before St Roque's was, and which now greatly helped the composition of the little landscape, and harmonised the new building with the old soil. St Roque's Cottage, by special intervention of Mr Wentworth, the perpetual curate, had dropped no intervening wall between its garden and those trees; but, not without many fears, had contented itself with a wooden paling on the side nearest the willows. Consequently, the slope of grass at that side, which Mrs Smith was too prudent to plant with anything that could be abstracted, was a pretty slope with the irregular willow shadows swept over it, thin, but still presenting a pale obstruction to the flood of sunshine on this special afternoon. There a little group was collected, in full enjoyment of the warmth and the light. Mrs Rider, still faded, but no longer travel-worn, sat farther up in the garden, on the green bench, which had been softened with cushions for her use, leisurely working at some piece of needlework, in lonely possession of the chrysanthemums and Michaelmas daisies round her; while on the grass, dropped over with yellow flecks of willow-leaves, lightly loosened by every passing touch of wind, sat Nettie, all brown and bright, working with the most rapid fingers at a child's frock, and "minding" with a corner of her eye the possessor of the same, the tiny Freddy, an imp of mischief uncontrollable by other hand or look than hers. A little lower down, poking into the invisible brook through the paling, was the eldest boy, silent from sheer delight in the unexpected pleasure of coating himself with mud without remark from Nettie. This unprecedented escape arose from the fact that Nettie had a visitor, a lady who had bent down beside her in a half-kneeling attitude, and was contemplating her with a mingled amaze and pity which intensified the prevailing expression of kindness in the mildest face in the world. It was Miss Wodehouse, in her soft dove-coloured dress and large soft checked shawl. Her mild eyes were fixed upon that brilliant brown creature, all buoyant and sparkling with youth. These wonderful young people perplexed Miss Wodehouse; here was another incomprehensible specimen—most incomprehensible perhaps of all that had ever crossed her mild elderly horizon with bewildering unintelligible light.

"My dear," said Miss Wodehouse, "things used to be very different when I was young. When we were girls we thought about our own pleasures—and—and vanities of all kinds," said the good woman, with a little sigh; "and, indeed, I can't think it is natural still to see you devoting yourself like this to your sister's family. It is wonderful; but dear, dear me! it isn't natural, Nettie, such self-devotion."

"I do wish you wouldn't speak!" said Nettie, with a sudden start—"self-devotion! stuff! I am only doing what must be done. Freddy can't go on wearing one frock for ever, can he—does it stand to reason? Would you have me sit idle and see the child's petticoats drop to pieces? I am a colonial girl—I don't know what people do in England. Where I was brought up we were used to be busy about whatever lay nearest to our hand."

"It isn't Freddy's frock," said Miss Wodehouse, with a little solemnity. "You know very well what I mean. And suppose you were to marry—what would happen supposing you were to marry, Nettie?"

"It is quite time enough to think of that when there is any likelihood of it happening," said Nettie, with a little toss of her head. "It is only idle people who have time to think of falling in love and such nonsense. When one is very busy it never comes into one's head. Why, you have never married, Miss Wodehouse; and when I know that I have everything I possibly could desire, why should I?"

Miss Wodehouse bent her troubled sweet old face over the handle of her parasol, and did not say anything for a few minutes. "It is all very well as long as you are young," she said, with a wistful look; "and somehow you young creatures are so much handier than we used to be. Our little Lucy, you know, that I can remember quite a baby—I am twice as old as she is," cried Miss Wodehouse, "and she is twice as much use in the world as I. Well, it is all very strange. But, dear, you know, *this* isn't natural all the same."

"It is dreadful to say so—it is dreadful to think so!" cried Nettie. "I know what you mean—not Freddy's frock, to be sure, but only one's whole life and heart. Should one desert the only people belonging to one in the world because one happens to have a little income and they have none? If one's friends are not very sensible, is that a reason why one should go and leave them? Is it right to make one's escape directly whenever one feels one is wanted? or what do you mean, Miss Wodehouse?" said the vehement girl. "That is what it comes to, you know. Do you imagine I had any choice about coming over to England when Susan was breaking her heart about her husband? could one let one's sister die, do you suppose? And now that they are all together, what choice have I? They can't do much for each other—there is actually nobody but me to take care of them all. You may say it is not natural, or it is not right, or anything you please, but what else can one do? That is the practical question," said Nettie, triumphantly. "If you will answer that, then I shall know what to say to you."

Miss Wodehouse gazed at her with a certain mild exasperation, shook her head, wrung her hands, but could find nothing to answer.

"I thought so," said Nettie, with a little outburst of jubilee; "that is how it always happens to abstract people. Put the practical question before them, and they have not a word to say to you. Freddy, cut the grass with the scissors, don't cut my trimmings; they are for your own frock, you little savage. If I were to say it was my duty and all that sort of stuff, you would understand me, Miss Wodehouse; but one only says it is one's duty when one has something disagreeable to do; and I am not doing anything disagreeable," added the little heroine, flashing those eyes which had confused Edward Rider—those brilliant, resolute, obstinate eyes, always with the smile of youth, incredulous of evil, lurking in them, upon her bewildered adviser. "I am living as I like to live."

There was a pause—at least there was a pause in the argument, but not in Nettie's talk, which ran on in an eager stream, addressed to Freddy, Johnnie, things in general. Miss Wodehouse pondered over the handle of her parasol. She had absolutely nothing to say; but, thoroughly unconvinced and exasperated at Nettie's logic, could not yet retire from the field.

"It is all very well to talk just now," said the gentle woman at last, retiring upon that potent feminine argument; "but, Nettie, think! If you were to marry——"

Miss Wodehouse paused, appalled by the image she herself had conjured up.

"Marrying is really a dreadful business, anyhow," she added, with a sigh; "so few people, you know, can, when they might. There is poor Mr Wentworth, who brought me here first; unless he gets preferment, poor fellow——. And there is Dr Rider. Things are very much changed from what they used to be in my young days."

"Is Dr Rider in the same dilemma? I suppose, of course, you mean Dr Edward," cried Nettie, with a little flash of mischievous curiosity. "Why? He has nobody but himself. I should like to know why he can't marry—that is, if anybody would have him—when he pleases. Tell me; you know he is my brother-in-law."

Miss Wodehouse had been thinking of Bessie Christian. She paused, partly for Dr Rider's sake, partly because it was quite contrary to decorum, to suppose that Bessie, now Mrs Brown, might possibly a year ago have married somebody else. She faltered a little in her answer. "A professional man never marries till he has a position," said Miss Wodehouse, abstractedly. Nettie lifted upon her, eyes that danced with mischief and glee.

"A profession is as bad as a family, then," said the little Australian. "I shall remember that next time you speak to me on this subject. I am glad to think Dr Edward, with all his prudence, is disabled too."

When Nettie had made this unguarded speech, she blushed; and suddenly, in a threatening and defiant manner, raised her eyes again to Miss Wodehouse's face. Why? Miss Wodehouse did not understand the look, nor put any significance into the words. She rose up from the grass, and said it was time for her to go. She went away, pondering in her own mind those singular new experiences of hers. She had never been called upon to do anything particular all her gentle life. Another fashion of woman might have found a call to action in the management of her father's house, or the education of her motherless young sister. But Miss Wodehouse had contented herself with loving Lucy—had suffered her to grow up very much as she would, without interference—had never taken a decided part in her life. When anything had to be done, to tell the truth, she was very inexpert—unready—deeply embarrassed with the unusual necessity. Nettie's case, so wonderfully different from anything she could have conceived, lay on her mind and oppressed her as she went home to Grange Lane.

As for Nettie herself, she took her work and her children indoors after a while, and tried on the new frock, and scolded and rehabilitated the muddy hero of the brook. Then, with those light fairy motions of hers, she spread the homely table for tea, called in Susan, sought Fred in his room up-stairs with a stinging word which penetrated even his callous mind, and made him for the moment ashamed of himself. Nettie bit her red lip till it grew white and bloodless as she turned from Fred's door. It was not hard to work for the children—to support and domineer over Susan; but it was hard for such an alert uncompromising little soul to tolerate that useless hulk—that heavy encumbrance of a man, for whom hope and life were dead. She bit her lip as she discharged her sharp stinging arrow at him through the half-opened door, and then went down singing, to take her place at the table which her own hands had spread—which her own purse supplied with bread. Nobody there showed the least consciousness of that latter fact; nobody fancied it was anything but natural to rely upon Nettie. The strange household demeaned itself exactly as if things were going on in the most regular and ordinary course. No wonder that spectators outside looked on with a wonder that could scarcely find expression, and half exasperated, half admiring, watched the astonishing life of the colonial girl.

Nobody watched it with half the amount of exasperation which concentrated in the bosom of Dr Rider. He gazed and noted and observed everything with a secret rage, indignation, and incredulity impossible to describe. He could not believe it even when it went on before his very eyes. Doctor though he was, and scientific, to a certain extent, Edward Rider would have believed in witchcraft—in some philtre or potion acting upon her mind, rather than in Nettie's voluntary folly. Was it folly? was it heroism? was it simple necessity, as she herself called it? Nobody could answer that question. The matter was as incomprehensible to Miss Wodehouse as to Dr Rider, but not of such engrossing interest. Bessie Christian, after all, grew tame in the Saxon composure of her beauty before this brown, sparkling, self-willed, imperious creature. To see her among her self-imposed domestic duties filled the doctor with a smouldering wrath against all surrounding her, which any momentary spark might set aflame.

CHAPTER VI.

Affairs went on in Carlingford with the usual commonplace pertinacity of human affairs. Notable events happened but seldom in anybody's life, and matters rolled back into their ordinary routine, or found a new routine for themselves after the ordinary course of humanity. After the extraordinary advent of Nettie and her strange household—after the setting-out of that wonderful little establishment, with all the amazed expectation it excited—it was strange to see how everything settled down, and how calmly the framework of common life took in that exceptional and half-miraculous picture. Lookers-on prophesied that it never could last—that in the very nature of things some sudden crisis or collapse must ensue, and the vain experiment prove a failure; but quiet nature and steady time prevailed over these moralists and their prophecies. The winter went on calmly day by day, and Nettie and her dependants became legitimate portions of Carlingford society. People ceased to wonder by degrees. Gradually the eyes of Carlingford grew accustomed to that dainty tiny figure sweeping along, by mere impulse of cheerful will and ceaseless activity, the three open-eyed staring children, the faded mother. Sometimes, indeed, Nettie, too clear of the necessity of her own exertions, and too simply bent upon her business, to feel any sentimental shame of her relations, was seen quickening the sluggish steps of Fred himself, who shuffled along by her side in a certain flush of self-disgust, never perceptible upon him under any other circumstances. Even Fred was duly moved by her vicinity. When he saw other people look at them, his bemused intellect was still alive enough to comprehend that people were aware of his dismal dependence upon that fairy creature, whom it was a shame to think of as the support not only of his deserted children, but of his own base comforts and idleness. But the spur, though it pricked, did not goad him into any action. When he got home, he took refuge in his room up-stairs, in the hazy atmosphere drugged with the heavy fumes of his pipe, and stretched his slovenly limbs on his sofa, and buried his confused faculties in his old novel. So he lived day by day, circumscribed in the most dangerous of his indulgences by Nettie's unhesitating strictures and rules, which nobody dared break, but unlimited in his indolence, his novel, and his pipe. That stifling fire, that close room, the ashes of the pipe on the table, the listless shabby figure on the sofa, were the most dismal part of the interior at St Roque's Cottage, so far as it appeared to the external eye. But it is doubtful whether Mrs Fred, spiteful and useless, with her poor health, her selfish love, her utter unreason, dawdling over trifling matters which she never completed; or the three children, entirely unrespectful of father and mother, growing up amid that wonderful subversion of the ordinary rules of nature, with some loyalty to Nettie, but no reverence in them, were not as appalling companions to live with. Nettie, however, did not consider the matter as a spectator might. She did not enter into it at all as a matter to be criticised; they simply belonged to her as they were. She knew their faults without loving them less, or feeling it possible that faults could make any difference to those bonds of nature. Fred, indeed, did afflict her lively impatient spirit;—she had tried to quicken him into life at first—she gave him up with a certain frank scorn now, and accepted her position. Thus he was to be all his life long this big cumberer of the ground. Nettie, valorous and simple, made up her mind to it. He was Fred—that was all that could be said on the subject; and, being Fred, belonged to her, and had to be cared for like the rest.

It all grew into a matter of routine as that winter glided along; outside and in, everybody came to take it for granted. Miss Wodehouse, who, with a yearning admiration of a creature so totally unlike herself, came often to visit Nettie, ceased to expostulate, almost ceased to wonder. Mr Wentworth no longer opened his fine eyes in amazement when that household was named. Mrs Smith, their landlady, calmly brought her bills to Nettie, and forgot that it was not the most natural thing in the world that she should be paid by Miss Underwood. The only persistent sceptic was the doctor. Edward Rider could not, would not, believe it. He who had so chafed under Fred's society, felt it beyond the bounds of human possibility that Nettie could endure him. He watched with an eagerness which he found it difficult to account for, to see the first symptoms of disgust which must ere long mark the failure of this bold but foolish venture. It occupied his mind a great deal more than was good for his own comfort; perhaps more than was best for his patients. Though he had few people to visit in that quarter of the town, his drag was seen to pass St Roque's Cottage most days in the week; and when urgent messages came for Dr Rider in the evening, his little groom always wended his way out through the special district of Dr Marjoribanks to find his master, if the doctor was not at home. Not that all this devotion assisted him much either in increase of friendship with his relations, or in verification of his auguries. The disgust of the young doctor, when he saw his brother's slovenly figure in his own chair, was nothing to his disgust now, when he saw that same form, so out of accordance with the neat little sitting-room which Nettie's presence made dainty and refined in its homeliness, lounging in Nettie's way. He could not bring himself to speak with ordinary patience to Fred; and Fred, obtuse as he was, perceived his brother's disgust and contempt, and resented it sullenly; and betrayed his resentment to the foolish wife, who sulked and said spiteful things to Edward. It was not a pleasant family group. As for Nettie, she was much too fully occupied to give her society or conversation to Dr Rider. She came and went while he was there, busy about a thousand things, always alert, decided, uncompromising—not disinclined to snub either Fred or Susan when opportunity offered, totally unconscious even of that delicacy with which a high fantastical

47

heroine of romance would have found it necessary to treat her dependants. It was this unconsciousness, above all, that irritated the doctor. If she had shown any feeling, he said to himself— if she had even been grandly aware of sacrificing herself and doing her duty—there would have been some consolation in it. But Nettie obstinately refused to be said to do her duty. She was doing her own will with an imperious distinctness and energy—having her own way—displaying no special virtue, but a determined wilfulness. Dr Rider was half disgusted with Nettie, to see how little disgust she showed of her companions. He was disappointed in her: he concluded to himself that she did not show that fine perception which he was disposed to expect from so dainty a little sprite. Yet, notwithstanding all these disappointed expectations, it is astonishing how he haunted that room where the society was so unattractive, and bore Mrs Fred's spiteful speeches, and suffered his eyes and his temper to be vexed beyond endurance by the dismal sight of his brother. The children, too, worried their unfortunate uncle beyond description. He did not dislike children: as a general rule, mothers in the other end of Carlingford, indeed, declared the doctor to be wonderfully tender and indulgent to his little patients: but those creatures, with their round staring eyes, the calm remarks they made upon their father's slovenly indolence and their mother's imbecility— their precocious sharp-sightedness and insubordination, moved Dr Rider with a sharp prevailing inclination, intensifying by times almost into action, to whip them all round, and banish the intolerable brats out of sight. Such was his unpaternal way of contemplating the rising hopes of his house. How Nettie could bear it all, was an unceasing marvel to the doctor. Yet, in spite of these disagreeables, he went to St Roque's all the same.

One of these winter evenings the doctor wended his way to St Roque's Cottage in a worse frame of mind than usual. It was a clear frosty night, very pleasant to be out in, though sharp and chill; such a night as brightens young eyes, and exhilarates young hearts, when all is well with them. Young Rider could hear his own footsteps echoing along the hard frost-bound road, and could not but wonder in himself, as he drew near the group of buildings which broke the solitude of the way, whether Nettie too might hear it, and *perhaps* recognise the familiar step. The shadow of St Roque's fell cold over him as he passed. Just from that spot the light in the parlour window of the cottage became perceptible to the wayfarer. A shadow crossed the blind as he came in sight—Nettie unquestionably. It occurred to Dr Rider to remember with very sharp distinctness at that moment, how Nettie's little shadow had dropped across the sunshine that first morning when he saw her in his own room. He quickened his step unawares—perhaps to-night Nettie might be more accessible than usual, less shut in and surrounded by her family. He pictured to himself, as he went past the willows, which rustled faintly with their long bare branches in the night air, that perhaps, as he was later than usual, Fred might have retired to his den up-stairs; and Susan might have gone to bear Fred company—who knows? and the children might be in bed, the dreadful little imps. And for once a half-hour's talk with the strange little head of the house might comfort the young doctor's fatigued mind and troubled heart.

For he was sadly fatigued and worn out. What with incessant occupation and distracted thoughts, this year had been a very exhausting one for the doctor. He had fagged on through the whole summer and autumn without any relaxation. He had chafed over Fred's presence for half of the year, and had been occupied for the other half with matters still more absorbing and exciting. Even now his mind was in a perpetual ferment, and no comforting spirit spoke quietness to his soul—no stout heart strengthened his—no lively intelligence animated his own to worthy doings. He was very cross and fretful, and knew himself to be so that particular evening—worried and in want of rest. What a chance, if perhaps he found Nettie, whose very provocations were somehow more interesting than other people's most agreeable and tranquillising efforts, all alone and at leisure! He went on with some palpitations of hope. As soon as he had entered the cottage, however, he found out the delusion he was under. The children were the first fact that presented itself to his senses; an uproar that pervaded the house, a novel tumult waking all the echoes; glimpses of flying figures pursuing each other with brushes and mops, and other impromptu weapons; one astride upon the banisters of the stairs, sliding down from top to bottom; another clinging now and then, in the pauses of the conflict, to the top of one of the doors, by which it swung back and forward. Terrible infants! there they all were in a complete saturnalia, the door of the parlour half open all the time, and no sound of Nettie's restraining voice. Only poor Mrs Smith standing helpless in successions of fright and exasperation, sometimes alarmed for life and limb, sometimes ready to give the little wretches over to all the penalties of poetic justice. The poor woman brightened a little when she perceived the sympathetic horror on the doctor's face.

"How's this?" exclaimed young Rider, with a sigh of dismay. Alas! however it was, no quiet imaginary conference, no soothing glimpse of Nettie, was practicable to-night. He grew sulky and ferocious under the thought. He seized the imp that hung on the door, and set it down summarily with a certain moral violence, unable to refrain from an admonitory shake, which startled its sudden scream into a quavering echo of alarm. "Do you want to break your neck, sir?" cried the wrathful uncle. Dr Rider, however, had to spring aside almost before the words were uttered to escape the encounter of a hearth-brush levelled at him by his sweet little niece. "How is this, Mrs Smith?" cried the startled visitor, with indignation, raising his voice sufficiently to be quite audible through the half-open door.

"Bless you, sir, Miss is gone out to tea—don't say nothing—I don't begrudge the poor young lady a bit of a holiday," whispered the frightened landlady under her breath; "but I can't never give in to it again. Their mamma never takes a bit of notice exceptin' when they're found fault with. Lord! to think how blind some folks is when it's their own. But the poor dear young lady, she's gone out for a little pleasure—only to Miss Wodehouse's, doctor," added Mrs Smith, looking up with a sudden start to catch the stormy expression on the doctor's face.

He made no reply to the troubled landlady. He pushed the children aside, and made a stride into the parlour. To be sure, if Nettie was not here, what a charming opportunity to make himself disagreeable, and give the other two a piece of his mind! Edward Rider was anything but perfect. He decided on that expedient with an angry satisfaction. Since he could not have Nettie, he would at least have this relief to his feelings, which was next best.

The room was full of smoke, which came in heavy puffs from Fred's pipe. He himself lay stretched on the little sofa; Nettie's sofa—Nettie's room—the place sacred in the doctor's heart to that bright little figure, the one redeeming presence in this dismal household. Mrs Fred sat dawdling opposite her husband over some wretched fancy-work. Eyes less prejudiced than those of Edward Rider might have imagined this a scene of coarse but not unpleasant domestic comfort. To him it was a disgusting picture of self-indulgence and selfish miserable enjoyment, almost vice. The very tobacco which polluted the atmosphere of her room was bought with Nettie's money. Pah! the doctor came in with a silent pale concentration of fury and disgust, scarcely able to compel himself to utter ordinary words of civility. His presence disturbed the pair in their stolen pleasure. Fred involuntarily put aside his pipe, and Mrs Fred made a little movement to remove from the table the glass from which her husband had been drinking; but both recollected themselves after a moment. The wife set down the glass with a little spiteful toss of her head; the husband, with that heated sullen flush upon his face, relighted his half-extinguished pipe, and put up again on the sofa the slovenly-slippered feet which at Edward's first appearance he had withdrawn from it. A sullen "How d'ye do?" was all the salutation that passed between them. *They* felt themselves found out; the visitor felt with rage and indignation that he had found them out. Defiant shame and resentment, spiteful passion and folly, on one side, encountered the gaze of a spectator outside whose opinion could not be mistaken, a known critic and possible spy. Little comfort could come from this strange reunion. They sat in uneasy silence for a few minutes, mutually ready to fly at each other. Mrs Fred, in her double capacity as a woman and a fool, was naturally the first to speak.

"Nettie's gone out to tea," said that good wife. "I daresay, Mr Edward, we should not have had the pleasure of seeing you here had you known that only Fred and I were at home. It is very seldom we have an evening to ourselves. It was too great a pleasure, I suppose, not to be disturbed."

"Susan, hold your confounded tongue," said the ungrateful Fred.

"I am sorry to disturb Mrs Rider," said Edward, with deadly civility. "I was not aware, indeed, of the domestic enjoyment I was likely to interrupt. But if you don't want your boys to break their necks, some one ought certainly to interfere outside there."

"That is exactly what I expected," said Mrs Fred. "My poor children can't have a little amusement, poor things, but somebody must interfere with it; and my poor Fred—perhaps you have some fault to find with him, Mr Edward? Oh, I can see it in your looks! so please take your advantage, now that there's nobody to be afraid of. I can tell you have ever so many pleasant things just on your lips to say."

"I wish you'd mind your own business, Susan," said her husband, who was not a fool. "Look after these imps there, and let me and Edward alone. Nettie's gone out, you understand. She's a wonderful creature, to be sure, but it's a blessed relief to get rid of her for a little. A man can't breathe under her sharp eyes," said Fred, half apologetic, half defiant, as he breathed out a puff of smoke.

Edward Rider stared at his brother, speechless with rage and indignation. He could have rushed upon that listless figure, and startled the life half out of the nerveless slovenly frame. The state of mingled resentment, disappointment, and disgust he was in, made every particular of this aggravating scene tell more emphatically. To see that heavy vapour obscuring those walls which breathed of Nettie—to think of this one little centre of her life, which always hitherto had borne in some degree the impress of her womanly image, so polluted and vulgarised, overpowered the young man's patience. Yet perhaps he of all men in the world had least right to interfere.

"How is it possible," burst forth the doctor all at once, "that you can live upon that creature, Fred? If you have the heart of a mouse in that big body of yours—if you are not altogether lost and degraded, how can you do it? And, by Jove, when all is done, to go and fill the only room she has—the only place you have left her—with this disgusting smoke and noise as soon as her back is turned! Good heaven! it sickens one to think of it. A fellow like you, as strong as any hodman, to let such a creature sacrifice herself to keep him in bread; and the only bit of a little place she can sit down in when she comes home—It's too much, you know—it's more than she ought to bear."

"And who are you, to meddle with us and our arrangements?" cried Mrs Fred. "My husband is in his own house. You would not take us into your house, Mr Edward——"

"Hold your confounded tongue, I tell you," said Fred, slowly gathering himself off the sofa. "You're a pretty fellow to speak, you are—that wouldn't lend a fellow a shilling to keep him from ruin. You had better remember where you are—in—in—as Susan says—my own house."

What outbreak of contempt might have come from the doctor's lips was fortunately lost at that moment, since a louder outcry than usual from outside, the screams of the children, and the wailings of the landlady, at length roused the mother to the length of going to the door. When she was gone the two brothers eyed each other threateningly. Fred, not without a certain intolerable sensation of shame, rose to knock his pipe upon the mantel-shelf among Nettie's pretty girlish ornaments. Somehow these aggravations of insult to her image drove Edward Rider desperate. He laid his hand on Fred's shoulder and shook him violently.

"Wake up! can't you wake up and see what you're about?" cried the doctor; "can't you show a little respect for her, at least? Look here, Fred Rider. I knew you could do anything shabby or mean, if it suited you. I knew you would consent to hang a burden on anybody that would take such a weight upon them; but, by Jove, I did not think you had the heart to insult her, after all. A man can't stand by and see that. Clear off your pipe and your brandy before she comes, or, as sure as I am made of flesh and blood, and not cast-iron——"

The doctor's threats were interrupted by the entrance of a woeful procession. Into the presence of the two brothers, eyeing each other with such lowering faces, Mrs Smith and her husband entered, carrying between them, with solemn looks, the unconscious Freddy, while his mother followed screaming, and his little brother and sister staring open-mouthed. It was some relief to the doctor's feelings, in the excitement of the moment, to rush to the window and throw it open, admitting a gust of chill December air, penetrating enough to search to the bones of the fireside loiterer. Fred was father enough to turn with anxiety to the child. But his trembling nervous fingers and bemused eyes could make nothing of the "case" thus so suddenly brought before him. He turned fiercely and vacantly upon his wife and demanded why everything was suffered to go to ruin when Nettie was away. Mrs Fred, screaming and terrified, began to recriminate. The pallid figure of the child on the table gave a certain air of squalid tragedy to the scene, to the sordid miseries of which the night air, coming in with a rush, chilling the group in their indoor dresses, and flickering the flame of the candles, added one other point of dismal accumulation. The child had dropped from his swing on the door, and was stunned with the fall. Both father and mother thought him dead in the excitement of the moment; but the accustomed and cooler eyes of the doctor perceived the true state of affairs. Edward Rider forgot his disgust and rage as he devoted himself to the little patient—not that he loved the child more, but that the habits of his profession were strong upon him. When he had succeeded in restoring the little fellow to consciousness, the doctor threw a professional glance of inquiry round him to see who could be trusted. Then, with a contemptuous shrug of his shoulders and impatient exclamation, turned back to the table. Fred, shivering and helpless, stood by the fire, uttering confused directions, and rubbing miserably his own flabby hands; his wife, crying, scolding, and incapable, stood at the end of the table, offering no assistance, but wondering when ever Nettie would come back. Dr Rider took the patient in his arms, and, beckoning Mrs Smith to go before him, carried the child up-stairs. There the good mistress of the cottage listened to all his directions, and promised devoutly to obey him—to keep the room quiet, if she could—to tell everything he had said to Miss Nettie. He did not enter the desecrated parlour again when he came down-stairs. What was the use? He was glad to go out and escape the chance of a fraternal struggle. He went out into the cold night air all thrilling with excitement and agitation. It was not wonderful that a scene so strange should rouse many impatient thoughts in the young man's mind; but the most intolerable of these had the most trifling origin. That Fred should have smoked his pipe in Nettie's sitting-room, when she was out of the way, was not, after all, considering Fred's character, a very wonderful circumstance, but it exasperated his brother to a greater extent than much more important matters. That aggravation entirely overpowered Edward Rider's self-control. It seemed the culmination of all the wrong and silent insolent injury inflicted upon Nettie. He saw the stain of those ashes on the little mantel-shelf, the rolling cloud of smoke in the room, and indignation burned yet higher and higher in his breast.

When the current of his thoughts was suddenly checked

and stimulated by the sound of voices on the road. Voices, one of which was Nettie's, one the lofty clerical accents of the Rev. Frank Wentworth. The two were walking arm-in-arm in very confidential colloquy, as the startled and jealous doctor imagined. What were these two figures doing together upon the road? why did Nettie lean on the arm of that handsome young clerical coxcomb? It did not occur to Dr Rider that the night was extremely dark, and that Nettie had been at Miss Wodehouse's, where the curate of St Roque's was a perpetual visitor. With a mortified and jealous pang, totally unreasonable and totally irresistible, Edward Rider, only a moment before so fantastically extreme in Nettie's defence—in the defence of Nettie's very "image" from all vulgar contact and desecration— strode past Nettie now without word or sign of recognition. She did not see him, as he observed with a throbbing heart; she was talking to young Mr Wentworth with all the haste and eagerness which Dr Rider had found so captivating. She never suspected who it was that brushed past her with breathless, exasperated impatience in the darkness. They went on past him, talking, laughing lightly, under the veil of night, quite indifferent as to who heard them, though the doctor did not think of that. He, unreasonably affronted, galled, and mortified, turned his back upon that house, which at this present disappointed moment did not contain one single thing or person which he could dwell on with pleasure; and, a hundred times more discontented, fatigued, and worn out—full of disgust with things in general, and himself and his own fate in particular—than he had been when he set out from the other end of Carlingford, went sulkily, and at a terrific pace, past the long garden-walls of Grange Lane, and all Dr Marjoribanks's genteel patients. When he had reached home, he found a message waiting him from an urgent invalid whose "case" kept the unhappy doctor up and busy for half the night. Such was the manner in which Edward Rider got through the evening—the one wonderful exceptional evening when Nettie went out to tea.

CHAPTER VII.

With the dawn of the morning, however, and the few hours' hurried rest which Edward Rider was able to snatch after his labours, other sentiments arose in his mind. It was quite necessary to see how the unlucky child was at St Roque's Cottage, and perhaps what Nettie thought of all that had occurred during her absence. The doctor bethought himself, too, that there might be very natural explanations of the curate's escort. How else, to be sure, could she have got home on a dark winter night through that lonely road? Perhaps, if he himself had been less impatient and ill-tempered, it might have fallen to his lot to supersede Mr Wentworth. On the whole, Dr Rider decided that it was necessary to make one of his earliest calls this morning at St Roque's.

It was a foggy frosty day, brightened with a red sun, which threw wintry ruddy rays across the mist. Dr Rider drew up somewhat nervously at the little Gothic porch. He was taken up-stairs to the bedroom where little Freddy lay moaning and feverish. A distant hum came from the other children in the parlour, the door of which, however, was fast closed this morning; and Nettie herself sat by the child's bedside—Nettie, all alert and vigorous, in the little room, which, homely as its aspect was, displayed even to the doctor's uninitiated glance a fastidious nicety of arrangement which made it harmonious with that little figure. Nettie was singing childish songs to solace the little invalid's retirement—the "fox that jumped up on a moonlight night," the "frog that would a-wooing go"—classic ditties of which the nursery never tires. The doctor, who was not aware that music was one of Nettie's accomplishments, stopped on the stairs to listen. And indeed she had not a great deal of voice, and still less science, Nettie's life having been too entirely

57

occupied to leave much room for such studies. Yet somehow her song touched the doctor's heart. He forgave her entirely that walk with the curate. He went in softly, less impatient than usual with her crazy Quixotism. A child—a sick child especially—was a bearable adjunct to the picture. A woman could be forgiven for such necessary ministrations—actually, to tell the truth, could be forgiven most follies she might happen to do, when one could have her to one's self, without the intervention of such dreary accessories as Susan and Fred.

"Thank you very much for your care of this child last night, Dr Edward," said the prompt Nettie, laying down the large piece of very plain needlework in her hand. "I always said, though you don't make a fuss about the children, that you were quite to be relied on if anything should happen. He is feverish, but he is not ill; and so long as I tell him stories and keep beside him, Freddy is the best child in the world."

"More people than Freddy might be willing to be ill under such conditions," said the doctor, complimentary, but rueful. He felt his patient's pulse, and prescribed for him with a softened voice. He lingered and looked round the room, which was very bare, yet somehow was not like any of the rooms in *his* house. How was it?—there were no ornaments about, excepting that tiny little figure with the little head overladen with such a wealth of beautiful hair. The doctor sighed. In this little sacred spot, where she was so clearly at her post—or at least at a post which no other was at hand to take—he could not even resent Nettie's self-sacrifice. He gave in to her here, with a sigh. "Since you think he is not ill to speak of, will you drive me and the other children into Carlingford, Dr Edward?" said the courageous Nettie. "It will be a pleasure for them, you know, and I shall be able to do my business without losing so much time; besides, I want to talk to you; I can see you will in your eyes. Go down, please, and talk to Mr Smith, who has got a headache or something, and wants to see you. You need not trouble yourself seeing Susan, who is cross, of course. I don't wonder at her being cross; it must be very shocking, you know, to feel one's self of no use, whatever happens. Thank you; I shall be ready in a minute, as soon as you have done talking to Mr Smith."

The doctor went down obediently, and in an unusual flutter of pleasure, to see the master of the cottage—totally indifferent to the ailments of the virtuous Smith, and thinking only of Nettie and that drive to Carlingford, where, indeed, he should not have gone, had he considered the merely abstract matters of business and duty, which led him entirely in a different direction. He was somewhat rudely recalled to himself when he went down-stairs. Smith had no headache, but only wanted to speak to the doctor about his lodgers, whose "ways" were sadly discomposing to himself and his wife.

"You saw how it was yourself last night, sir," said the troubled landlady. "Them hangings—you know the smoke goes through and through them. After leaving all the windows open this frosty morning, and a draught enough to give you your death, the place smells like I don't know what. If it wasn't for Miss I wouldn't put up with it for a day; and the gentleman's own room, doctor; if you was just to go in and see it—just put your head in and say good morning—you'd believe me."

"I know all about it," said the doctor; "but Miss Underwood, Mrs Smith—?"

"There's where it is, sir," said the landlady. "I can't find it in my heart to say a word to Miss. To see how she do manage them all, to be sure! but for all that, doctor, it stands to reason as one can't spoil one's lodgings for a family as may be gone to-morrow—not except it's considered in the rent. It's more natural-like to speak to a gentleman like you as knows the world, than to a young lady as one hasn't a word to say against—the handiest, liveliest, managingest! Ah, doctor, she'd make a deal different a wife from her sister, that young lady would! though it isn't my part to say nothink, considering all things, and that you're relations, like; but Smith and me are both o' one mind about it, Dr Rider—unless it's considered in the rent, or the gentleman drops smoking, or——"

"I hear Miss Underwood coming down-stairs," cried young Rider. "Next time I come we'll arrange it all. But not a word to *her*, remember—not a syllable; and go up-stairs and look after that poor child, there's a good soul—she trusts you while she is gone, and so do I. There, there! another time. I'll take the responsibility of satisfying you, Mrs Smith," said the doctor, in a prodigious hurry, ready to promise anything in this incautious moment, and bolting out of their little dark back-room, which the local architect's mullions had converted into a kind of condemned cell. Nettie stood at the door, all ready for her expedition to Carlingford, with her two children, open-eyed and calmly inquisitive, but no longer noisy. Mrs Fred was standing sulky at the parlour door. The doctor took off his hat to her as he helped Nettie into the front seat of the drag, but took care not to approach nearer. The children were packed in behind, under charge of the little groom, and, with an exhilarating sensation of lawlessness in the present pleasure, Dr Rider turned his back upon his duty and the patient who expected him a mile on the other side of St Roque's, and drove, not too rapidly, into Carlingford.

"Mrs Smith was talking to you of us," said Nettie, flashing her penetrating eyes upon the confused doctor. "I know she was—I could see it in her face this morning, and in yours when you came out of her room. Dreadful little dungeon, is it not? I wonder what the man meant, to build such a place. Do they want to turn us out, Dr Edward, or do they want more rent? I am not surprised, I am sure, after last night. Was it not odious of Fred to go and smoke in the parlour, the only place we can have tidy? But it is no use speaking to him, you know; nor to Susan either, for that matter. Married people do stand up for each other so when you say a word, however they may fight between themselves. But is it more rent they want, Dr Edward? for I can't afford more rent."

"It is an abominable shame—you oughtn't to afford anything. It is too dreadful to think of!" cried the angry doctor, involuntarily touching his horse with his whip in the energy of the moment, though he was indeed in no hurry to reach Carlingford.

"Hush," said Nettie, lifting her tiny hand as though to put it to his incautious mouth, which, indeed, the doctor would not have objected to. "We shall quarrel on that subject if you say anything more, so it is better to stop at once. Nobody has a right to interfere with me; this is my business, and no one else has anything to do with it."

"You mistake," cried the doctor, startled out of all his prudences; "it ought to be my business quite as much as it is yours."

Nettie looked at him with a certain careless scorn of the inferior creature—"Ah, yes, I daresay; but then you are only a man," said Nettie; and the girl elevated that pretty drooping head, and flashed a whole torrent of brilliant reflections over the sombre figure beside her. He felt himself glow under the sudden radiance of the look. To fancy this wilful imperious creature a meek self-sacrificing heroine, was equally absurd and impossible. Was there any virtue at all in that dauntless enterprise of hers? or was it simple determination to have her own way?

"But not to quarrel," said Nettie; "for indeed you are the only person in the world I can say a word to about the way things are going on," she added with a certain momentary softening of voice and twinkling of her eyelid, as if some moisture had gathered there. "I think Fred is in a bad way. I think he is muddling his brains with that dreadful life he leads. To think of a man that could do hundreds of things living like that! A woman, you know, can only do a thing or two here and there. If it were not wicked to say so, one would think almost that Providence forgot sometimes, and put the wrong spirit into a body that did not belong to it. Don't you think so? When I look at Fred I declare sometimes I could take hold of him and give him a good shake, and ask him what he means; and then it all seems so useless the very idea of expecting him to feel anything. I want to know what you said to him last night."

"Not much—not half so much as I meant to have said. To see

him polluting your room!" cried the doctor, with a flush growing on his face, and breaking off abruptly, not quite able to conclude the sentence. Nettie gave him a shy upward glance, and grew suddenly crimson too.

"Did you mind?" said Nettie, with a momentary timidity, against the unexpected charm of which the unhappy doctor fell defenceless; then holding out her tiny hand to him with shy frankness, "Thank you for caring so much for me," said the dauntless little girl, resolute not to perceive anything which could not be fully spoken out.

"Caring so much! I must speak to you; we can't go on like this, Nettie," cried the doctor, holding fast the little unfaltering hand.

"Oh, here is the place I am going to. Please don't; people might not understand,—though we are brother and sister in a kind of a way," said the little Australian. "Please, Dr Edward, we must get out here."

For a moment Edward Rider hesitated with a wild intention of urging his horse forward and carrying her off anywhere, out of Carlingford, out of duty and practice and responsibility, and all those galling restraints of life which the noonday light and everyday sounds about brought in with so entire a discord to break up this momentary hallucination. For half a minute only the doctor lingered on the borders of that fairyland where time and duty are not, but only one ineffable moment always passing, never past. Then with a long sigh, the breath of which dispersed a whole gleaming world of visionary delights, he got down doggedly on the commonplace pavement. Ah, what a descent it was! the moment his foot touched these vulgar flags, he was once more the hard-worked doctor at everybody's command, with a fretful patient waiting for him a mile beyond St Roque's; and all these dazzling moments, which had rapt the unfortunate young fellow into another world, were so much time lost to the prose figure that had to help Nettie down and let her go, and betake himself soberly about his own business. Perhaps Nettie felt it a little disenchanting too, when she was dropped upon the bare street, and went into the common shop, and saw the doctor's drag flash off in the red frosty sunshine with a darting movement of exasperation and impatience on the part of its aggravated driver. For once in her life Nettie felt disposed to be impatient with the children, who, unceremoniously ejected from their perch behind, were not in the most obedient frame of mind. The two young people possibly agreed in their mutual sentiment of disgust with other people's society just at that moment. However, there was no help for it. Dr Rider galloped his horse to his patient's door, and took it out of that unlucky individual, who was fortunately strong enough to be able to bear sharp practice. Nettie, when she had made her little purchases, walked home smartly to sing "The fox jumped up on a moonlight night" to little Freddy in his bedroom. This kind of interlude, however, as all young men and maidens ought to be aware, answers much better in the evening, when a natural interval of dreams interposes between it and the common work of existence. Nettie decided, thinking on it, that this would never do. She made up her mind not to have any more drives with the doctor. There was no telling what such proceedings might lead to. They were distinctly incompatible with the more serious business of her life.

CHAPTER VIII.

Such a parting, however, is sadly apt to lead to future meetings. Notwithstanding his smouldering quarrel with Fred, which was always ready to burst out afresh, Dr Rider would not give up coming to St Roque's. He came to some clandestine arrangement with Mrs Smith, of which nobody ever was aware, and which he himself was rather ashamed of than otherwise; and he attended Freddy with the most dutiful exactness till the child was quite restored. But all this time Nettie put on a coat of armour, and looked so thoroughly unlike herself in her unusual reserve and propriety, that the doctor was heartily discouraged, and could go no further. Besides, it would not be positively correct to assert that—though he would gladly have carried her off in the drag anywhere, to the end of the world, in the enchantment of the moment—he was just as ready to propose setting up a new household, with Fred and his family hanging on to it as natural dependants. That was a step the doctor was not prepared for. Some people are compelled to take the prose concerns of life into full consideration even when they are in love, and Edward Rider was one of these unfortunate individuals. The boldness which puts everything to the touch to gain or lose was not in this young man. He had been put to hard encounters enough in his day, and had learned to trust little to chance or good fortune. He did not possess the boldness which disarms an adverse fate, nor that confidence in his own powers which smooths down wounded pride, and accounts even for failure. He was, perhaps it is only right to say, not very capable of heroism: but he was capable of seeing the lack of the heroic in his own composition, and of feeling bitterly his own self-reproaches, and the remarks of the world, which is always so ready to taunt the very cowardice it creates. After that moment in which he could have dared anything for her and with her, it is sad to be obliged to admit that perhaps Dr Edward too, like Nettie, withdrew a little from that climax of feeling. Not that his heart grew colder or his sentiments changed; but only that, in sight of the inevitable result, the poor young fellow paused and pondered, obeying the necessity of his nature. People who jump at conclusions, if they have to bear the consequences of folly often enough, are at least spared those preliminary heartaches. Dr Rider, eager as love and youth could make him, was yet incapable of shutting his eyes to the precipice at his feet. That he despised himself for doing so, did not make the matter easier. These were the limits of his nature, and beyond them he could not pass.

Accordingly matters went on in this dangerous fashion for many weeks longer. The fire smouldered, strengthening its pent-up flames. Day by day malicious sprites of thought went out behind Dr Rider in his drag, leading him into the wildest calculations, the most painful complication of schemes. If Fred and his family could only be persuaded to return to Australia, his brother thought—if any bribe within Edward's means could tempt the ruined man to such a step; and when he was there, why there was Providence to take care of the helpless unlovely household, and necessity might compel the wretched father to work for his children. Such were the vain projects that revolved and fermented through the doctor's agitated brain as he went among his patients. Luckily he had a very favourable and well-disposed lot of sick people at that crisis—they all got well in spite of the doctor, and gave their own special cases and his anxiety all the credit for his grave looks; and all these half-finished streets and rough new roads in the east end of Carlingford were sown thick with the bootless suggestions of Dr Rider's love and fears. The crop did not show upon the vulgar soil, but gave lurking associations to every half-built street corner which he passed in his rounds many a day after, and served at this present momentous era to confuse doubly the chaos of his thoughts.

At last one night the crisis came. Spring had begun to show faintly in the lengthening days—spring, that so often belies itself, and comes with a serpent's tooth. Dr Rider on that particular day had met Dr Marjoribanks at some meeting convened in the interests of Carlingford. The old physician had been very gracious and cordial to the young one—had spoken of his own declining health, of his possible retirement, of the excellent prospects which a rising young man in their profession had in Carlingford; and, finally, had asked Dr Rider to go with him next day to see an interesting patient, and advise as to the treatment of the case.

The young doctor was more pleased than he could or would have told any one; and, with a natural impulse, seized the earliest moment to direct his steps towards St Roque's.

It was twilight when Dr Edward went down the long and rather tiresome line of Grange Lane. These garden-walls, so delicious in their bowery retirements within, were not interesting outside to the pedestrian. But the doctor's attention was so speedily riveted on two figures eagerly talking near Mr Wodehouse's garden-door, that the long sweep of wall seemed but a single step to him as he hurried along. Those two figures were unquestionably Nettie for one, and Mr Wentworth for another. Handsome young coxcomb, with all his Puseyitical pretences! Was Lucy Wodehouse not enough for him, that he must have Nettie too? Dr Rider hurried forward to interrupt that meeting. He was actually turning with her, walking slowly back again the very way he had just come! Edward's blood boiled in his impatient veins. He swept along in a whirlwind of sudden wrath. When he came up to them Nettie was talking low, and the curate's lofty head was bent to hear her in a manner which, it is probable, Lucy Wodehouse would no more have admired than Edward Rider. They came to a sudden pause when he joined them, in that particular conversation. The doctor's dread civility did not improve matters. Without asking himself what cause he had, this amiable young man plunged into the wildest jealousy without pause or interval. He bestowed upon

Nettie the most cutting looks, the most overwhelming politeness. When the three had marched solemnly abreast down the road for some few minutes, the curate, perhaps with an intuition of fellow-feeling, perceiving how the matter was, stopped short and said good-bye. "I will make inquiries, and let you know next time I pass the cottage," said Mr Wentworth; and he and the doctor took off their hats, not without deadly thoughts on one side at least. When the young clergyman left them, Nettie and her sulky cavalier went on in silence. That intrepid little woman was not in her usual spirits, it appeared. She had no talk for Dr Edward any more than he had for her. She carried a multiplicity of little parcels in her hands, and walked with a certain air of fatigue. The doctor walked on, stealing silent looks at her, till his heart melted. But the melting of his heart displayed itself characteristically. He would not come down from his elevation without suffering her to see how angry he was.

"I fear I interrupted an interesting conversation—I that have so little hope of equalling Mr Wentworth. Priests are always infallible with women," said the doctor, betraying his ill-temper in vulgar sneers.

"I was asking him for some one to teach the boys," said Nettie. "Johnnie ought to have his education attended to now. Mr Wentworth is very good-tempered, Dr Edward. Though he was just going to knock at Miss Wodehouse's door when I met him, he offered, and would have done it if you had not come up, to walk home with me. Not that I wanted anybody to walk home with me; but it was very kind," said Nettie, with rising spirit.

"I am afraid I am a very poor substitute for Mr Wentworth," said the jealous doctor, "and I don't pretend to be kind. But I am surprised to find Miss Underwood walking so late. This is not a road for a lady by herself."

"You know I don't mind in the least for the road," said Nettie, with a little indignation. "How wonderfully cross you are sometimes! If you are going as far as the Cottage," she added, with a little sigh of fatigue, "will you please carry some of these things for me! I could not get out sooner, I have been so busy to-day. It is wonderful how much needlework it takes to keep three children going, and how many little jobs there are to do. If you take this parcel, carry it carefully, please: it is something for my bonnet. There! Don't be absurd. I am quite able to walk by myself, thank you—I'd rather, please!"

This remonstrance was called forth by the fact that the relenting doctor, much moved by having the parcels confided to his care, had drawn the little hand which gave them within his arm, a proceeding which Nettie distinctly disapproved of. She withdrew her hand quickly, and walked on with much dignity by his side.

"I can carry your parcels," said Edward, after a little pause, "but you will not let me help yourself. You take the heaviest burdens upon your shoulders, and then will have no assistance in bearing them. How long are these children of Fred's—detestable little imps!—to work you to death?"

"You are speaking of *my* children, sir!" cried Nettie, with a little blaze of resentment. "But you don't mean it, Dr Edward," she said, a moment after, in a slightly coaxing tone. "You are tired and cross after your day's work. Perhaps it will be best, if you are very cross, not to come down all the way to the Cottage, thank you. I don't want you to quarrel with Fred."

"Cross! Nettie, you are enough to drive twenty men distracted!" cried the poor doctor. "You know as well as I do what I have been dying to say to you these three months past; and to see you go on with these confounded children without so much as a glance for a fellow who——"

"Don't speak like that," cried Nettie, with brilliant female instinct; "you'll be sorry for it after; for you know, Dr Edward, you have *not* said anything particular to me these three months past."

This touch gave the last exasperation to the agitated mind of the doctor. He burst forth into a passionate outbreak of love and anger, curiously mingled, but too warm and real to leave

Nettie much coolness of observation under the circumstances. She took the advantage over him which a woman naturally does in such a case. She went on softly, trembling sufficiently to her own consciousness, but not to his, suffering him to pour out that torrent without interruption. She made no answer till the whole agitated self-disclosure was complete. In the interval she got a little command of herself, and was able to speak when it came to her turn.

"Dr Edward," said Nettie, solemnly, "you know it is impossible. If we cared for each other ever so much, what could we do? I am not free to—to make any change; and I know very well, and so do you, that you never could put up with Fred and Susan and the children, were things as you say ten times over. I don't mean I don't believe you. I don't mean I might not have been pleased had things been different. But you know it is just plainly impossible. You know your own temper and your own spirit—and perhaps you know mine as well. No, no—we cannot manage it anyhow, Dr Edward," said Nettie, with a little sigh.

"Is this all you have to say to me?" cried the astonished lover.

"I am sure I do not know what else to say," said Nettie, with matter-of-fact distinctness. "I don't need to enter into all the business again, and tell you how things stand; you know as well as I do. One may be sorry, but one must do what one has to do all the same."

A painful pause followed. Nettie, with all her feminine acuteness, could not divine that this calm way of treating a business which had wrought her companion into such a pitch of passion, was the most humiliating and mortifying possible to a man in whose bosom love and pride were so combined. He tried to speak more than once, but could not. Nettie said nothing more—she was uneasy, but secure in the necessity of her own position. What else could she do or say?

"Then, I presume, this is my answer," said the doctor, at last, gulping an amount of shame and anger which Nettie could not conceive of, and which the darkness concealed from her sight.

"Oh, Dr Edward, what can I say?" cried the girl; "you know it all as well as I do. I cannot change it with a word. I am very, very sorry," said Nettie, faltering and startled, waking to a sudden perception of the case all at once, by reason of catching a sudden gleam of his eyes. They came to a dead stop opposite each other, she half frightened and confused, he desperate with love and rage and mortification. By this time they had almost reached the cottage door.

"Don't take the trouble to be sorry. I'll—oh, I'll get over it!" cried the doctor, with a sneer at himself and his passion, which came out of the bitterness of his heart. Then, after a pause— "Nettie!" cried the young man—"Nettie! do you see what you are doing?—do you choose Fred and those wretched imps instead of your own life and mine? You are not so indifferent as you think you are. We shall never get over it, neither you nor me. Nettie, once for all, is this all you have to say?"

"If I were to say all the words in the language," said Nettie, after a pause, with a breathless indistinctness and haste, "words will not change *things* if we should break our hearts."

The open door, with the light shining out from it, shone upon them at that moment, and Mrs Smith waiting to let the young lady in. Neither of the two dared face that sudden gleam. The doctor laid down his parcels on the step, muttered something, which she could not distinguish, into Nettie's agitated ear, and vanished back again into the darkness. Only now was Nettie awaking to the sense of what had happened, and its real importance. Perhaps another minute, another word, might have made a difference— that other word and minute that are always wanting. She gazed out after him blankly, scarcely able to persuade herself that it was all over, and then went in with a kind of stupefied, stunned sensation, not to be described. Edward Rider heard the door shut in the calm silence, and swore fierce oaths in his heart over her composure and cold-heartedness. As usual, it was the woman who had to face the light and observation, and to veil her trouble. The man rushed back into the darkness, smarting with wounds which fell as severely upon his pride as upon his heart. Nettie went in, suddenly conscious that the world was changed, and that she had entered upon another life.

CHAPTER IX.

Another life and a changed world! What small matters sometimes bring about that sudden disenchantment! Two or three words exchanged without much thought—one figure disappearing out of the landscape—and, lo! all the prismatic colours have faded from the horizon, and blank daylight glares upon startled eyes! Nettie had not, up to this time, entertained a suspicion of how distinct a place the doctor held in her limited firmament—she was totally unaware how much exhilaration and support there was in his troubled, exasperated, impatient admiration. Now, all at once, she found it out. It was the same life, yet it was different. Her occupations were unchanged, her surroundings just what they used to be. She had still to tolerate Fred, to manage Susan, to superintend with steady economy all the expenditure of the strange little household. The very rooms and aspect of everything was the same; yet had she been suddenly transported back again to the Antipodes, life could not have been more completely changed to Nettie. She recognised it at once with some surprise, but without any struggle. The fact was too clearly apparent to leave her in any doubt. Nobody but herself had the slightest insight into the great event which had happened—nobody could know of it, or offer Nettie any sympathy in that unforeseen personal trial. In her youth and buoyant freshness, half contemptuous of the outside troubles which were no match for her indomitable heart, Nettie had been fighting against hard external circumstances for a great part of her valorous little life, and had not hesitated to take upon herself the heaviest burdens of outside existence. Such struggles are not hard when one's heart is light and sound. With a certain splendid youthful scorn of all these labours and drudgeries,

Nettie had gone on her triumphant way, wearing her bonds as if they were ornaments. Suddenly, without any premonition, the heart had died out of her existence. A personal blow, striking with subtle force into that unseen centre of courage and hope, had suddenly disabled Nettie. She said not a word on the subject to any living creature—if she shed any tears over it, they were dropped in the darkness, and left no witness behind; but she silently recognised and understood what had happened to her. It was not that she had lost her lover—it was not that the romance of youth had glimmered and disappeared from before her eyes. It was not that she had ever entered, even in thought, as Edward Rider had done, into that life, glorified out of common existence, which the two could have lived together. Such was not the form which this extraordinary loss took to Nettie. It was her personal happiness, wonderful wine of life, which had suddenly failed to the brave little girl. Ah, the difference it made! Labours, disgusts, endurances of all kinds: what cannot one undertake so long as one has that cordial at one's heart? When the endurance and the labour remain, and the cordial is gone, it is a changed world into which the surprised soul enters. This was what had happened to Nettie. Nobody suspected the sudden change which had passed upon everything. The only individual in the world who could have divined it, had persuaded himself in a flush of anger and mortification that she did not care. He consoled himself by elaborate avoidance of that road which led past St Roque's—by bows of elaborate politeness when he encountered her anywhere in the streets of Carlingford—by taking a sudden plunge into such society as was open to him in the town, and devoting himself to Miss Marjoribanks, the old physician's daughter. Nettie was not moved by these demonstrations, which showed her sway still undiminished over the doctor's angry and jealous heart. She did not regard the petulant shows of pretended indifference by which a more experienced young woman might have consoled herself. She had enough to do, now that the unsuspected stimulus of her life was withdrawn for the moment, to go on steadily without making any outward show of it. She had come to the first real trial of her strength and worthiness. And Nettie did not know what a piece of heroism she was enacting, nor that the hardest lesson of youthful life—how to go on stoutly without the happiness which that absolute essence of existence demands and will not be refused—was being taught her now. She only knew it was dull work just for the moment—a tedious sort of routine, which one was glad to think could not last for ever; and so went on, the steadfast little soul, no one being any the wiser, upon that suddenly-clouded, laborious way.

It is sad to be obliged to confess that Dr Rider's conduct was nothing like so heroical. He, injured and indignant and angry, thought first of all of revenging himself upon Nettie—of proving to her that he would get over it, and that there were women in the world more reasonable than herself. Dr Marjoribanks, who had already made those advances to the doctor which that poor young fellow had gone to carry the news of, not without elation of heart, on that memorable night, to St Roque's, asked Edward to dinner a few days after; and Miss Marjoribanks made herself very agreeable, with just that degree of delicate regard and evident pleasure in his society which is so soothing when one has met with a recent discomfiture. Miss Marjoribanks, it is true, was over thirty, and by no means a Titania. Edward Rider, who had retired from the field in Bessie Christian's case, and whom Nettie had rejected, asked himself savagely why he should not make an advantageous marriage now, when the chance offered. Old Marjoribanks's practice and savings, with a not unagreeable, rather clever, middle-aged wife—why should he not take it into consideration? The young doctor thought of that possibility with a certain thrill of cruel pleasure. He said to himself that he would make his fortune, and be revenged on Nettie. Whenever there was a chance of Nettie hearing of it, he paid the most devoted attentions to Miss Marjoribanks. Ready gossips took it up and made the matter public. Everybody agreed it would be an admirable arrangement. "The most sensible thing

I've heard of for years—step into the old fellow's practice, and set himself up for life—eh, don't you think so?—that's my opinion," said Mr Wodehouse. Mr Wodehouse's daughters talked over the matter, and settled exactly between themselves what was Miss Marjoribanks's age, and how much older she was than her supposed suitor—a question always interesting to the female mind. And it was natural that in these circumstances Nettie should come to hear of it all in its full details, with the various comments naturally suggesting themselves thereupon. What Nettie's opinion was, however, nobody could ever gather; perhaps she thought Dr Edward was justified in putting an immediate barrier between himself and her. At all events, she was perfectly clear upon the point that it could not have been otherwise, and that no other decision was possible to herself.

The spring lagged on, accordingly, under these circumstances. Those commonplace unalterable days, varied in nothing but the natural fluctuations of making and mending,—those evenings with Fred sulky by the fire—always sulky, because deprived by Nettie's presence of his usual indulgences; or if not so, then enjoying himself after his dismal fashion in his own room, with most likely Susan bearing him company, and the little maiden head of the house left all by herself in the solitary parlour,— passed on one by one, each more tedious than the other. It seemed impossible that such heavy hours could last, and prolong themselves into infinitude, as they did; but still one succeeded another in endless hard procession. And Nettie shed back her silky load of hair, and pressed her tiny fingers on her eyes, and went on again, always dauntless. She said to herself, with homely philosophy, that this could not last very long; not with any tragical meaning, but with a recognition of the ordinary laws of nature which young ladies under the pressure of a first disappointment are not apt to recur to. She tried, indeed, to calculate in herself, with forlorn heroism, how long it might be expected to last, and, though she could not fix the period, endeavoured to content herself with the thought that things must eventually fall into their natural condition. In the mean time it was slow and tedious work enough—but they did pass one after another, these inevitable days.

One night Nettie was sitting by herself in the parlour busy over her needlework. Fred and his wife, she thought, were up-stairs. They had left her early in the evening,—Susan to lie down, being tired—Fred to his ordinary amusements. It was a matter of course, and cost Nettie no special thought. After the children went to bed, she sat all by herself, with her thread and scissors on the table, working on steadily and quietly at the little garment she was making. Her needle flew swift and nimbly; the sleeve of her dress rustled as she moved her arm; her soft breath went and came: but for that regular monotonous movement, and those faint steady sounds of life, it might have been a picture of domestic tranquillity and quiet, and not a living woman with aches in her heart. It did not matter what she was thinking. She was facing life and fortune—indomitable, not to be discouraged. In the silence of the house she sat late over her needlework, anxious to have some special task finished. She heard the mistress of the cottage locking up, but took no notice of that performance, and went on at her work, forgetting time. It got to be very silent in the house and without; not a sound in the rooms where everybody was asleep; not a sound outside, except an occasional rustle of the night wind through the bare willow-branches—deep night and not a creature awake but herself, sitting in the heart of that intense and throbbing silence. Somehow there was a kind of pleasure to Nettie in the isolation which was so impossible to her at other hours. She sat rapt in that laborious quiet as if her busy fingers were under some spell.

When suddenly she heard a startled motion up-stairs, as if some one had got up hastily; then a rustling about the room overhead, which was Susan's room. After a while, during which Nettie, restored by the sound to all her growing cares, rose instantly to consideration of the question, What had happened now? the door above was stealthily opened, and a footstep came softly down the stair. Nettie put down her work and listened breathlessly. Presently Susan's head peeped in at the parlour door. After all, then, it was only some restlessness of Susan's. Nettie took up her work, impatient, perhaps almost disappointed, with the dead calm in which nothing ever happened. Susan came in stealthy, pale, trembling with cold and fright. She came forward to the table in her white night-dress like a faded ghost. "Fred has never come in," said Susan, in a shivering whisper; "is it very late? He promised he would only be gone an hour. Where *can* he have gone? Nettie, Nettie, don't sit so quiet and stare at me. I fell asleep, or I should have found it out sooner; all the house is locked up, and he has never come in."

"If he comes we can unlock the house," said Nettie. "When did he go out, and why didn't you tell me? Of course I should have let Mrs Smith know, not to frighten her; but I told Fred pretty plainly last time that we could not do with such hours. It will make him ill if he does not mind. Go to bed, and I'll let him in."

"Go to bed! it is very easy for you to say so; don't you know it's the middle of the night, and as dark as pitch, and my husband out all by himself?" cried Susan. "Oh, Fred, Fred! after all the promises you made, to use me like this again! Do you think I can go up-stairs and lie shivering in the dark, and imagining all sorts of dreadful things happening to him? I shall stay here with you till he comes in."

Nettie entered into no controversy. She got up quietly and fetched a shawl and put it round her shivering sister; then sat down again and took up her needlework. But Susan's excited nerves could not bear the sight of that occupation. The rustle of Nettie's softly-moving hand distracted her. "It sounds always like Fred's step on the way," said the fretful anxious woman. "Oh, Nettie, Nettie! do open the end window and look out; perhaps he is looking for the light in the windows to guide him straight! It is so dark! Open the shutters, Nettie, and, oh, do look out and see! Where do you suppose he can have gone to? I feel such a pang at my heart, I believe I shall die."

"Oh, no, you will not die," said Nettie. "Take a book and read, or do something. We know what is about the worst that will happen to Fred. He will come home *like that* you know, as he did before. We can't mend it, but we need not break our hearts over it. Lie down on the sofa, and put up your feet and wrap the shawl round you if you won't go to bed. I can fancy all very well how it will be. It is nothing new, Susan, that you should break your heart."

"It's you that have no feeling. Oh, Nettie, how hard you are! I don't believe you know what it is to love anybody," said Susan. "Hark! is that some one coming now?"

They thought some one was coming fifty times in the course of that dreadful lingering night. Nobody came; the silence closed in deeper and deeper around the two silent women. All the world—everything round about them, to the veriest atom—seemed asleep. The cricket had stopped his chirrup in the kitchen, and no mouse stirred in the slumbering house. By times Susan dozed on the sofa, shivering, notwithstanding her shawl, and Nettie took up her needlework for the moment to distract her thoughts. When Susan started from these snatches of slumber, she importuned her sister with ceaseless questions and entreaties. Where had he gone?—where did Nettie imagine he could have gone?—and oh! would she go to the window and look out to see if any one was coming, or put the candle to the window to guide him, if perhaps he might have lost the way? At last the terrible pale dawn came in and took the light out of Nettie's candle. The two looked at each other, and acknowledged with a mutual start that the night was over. They had watched these long hours through with sentiments very different; now a certain thrill of sympathy drew Nettie nearer to her sister. It was daylight again, remorseless and uncompromising, and where was Fred, who loved the darkness? He had little money and less credit in the limited place where himself and his story were known. What could have become of him? Nettie acknowledged that there was ground for anxiety. She folded up her work and put out her candle, and promptly took into consideration what she could do.

"If you will go to bed, Susan, I shall go out and look for him," said Nettie. "He might have stumbled in the field and fallen asleep. Men have done such things before now, and been none the worse for it. If you will go and lie down, I'll see after it, Susan. Now it's daylight, you know, no great harm can happen to him. Come and lie down, and leave me to look for Fred."

"But you don't know where to go, and he won't like to have you going after him. Nettie, send to Edward," said Susan; "he ought to come and look after his brother: he ought to have done it all through, and not to have left us to manage everything; and he hasn't even been to see us for ever so long. But send to Edward, Nettie—it's his business. For Fred won't like to have you going after him, and you don't know where to go."

"Fred must have me going after him whether he likes it or no," said Nettie, sharply, "and I shall not send to Dr Edward. You choose to insult him whenever you can, and then you think it is his business to look after his brother. Go to bed, and leave it to me. I can't leave you shivering here, to catch something, and be ill, and laid up for weeks. I want to get my bonnet on, and to see you in bed. Make haste, and come up-stairs with me."

Susan obeyed with some mutterings of inarticulate discontent. The daylight, after the first shock of finding that the night was really over, brought some comfort to her foolish heart. She thought that as Nettie said "no more harm" could come to him, he must be sleeping somewhere, the foolish fellow. She thought most likely Nettie was right, and that she had best go to bed to consume the weary time till there could be something heard of him; and Nettie, of course, would find it all out.

Such was the arrangement accordingly. Susan covered herself up warm, and lay thinking all she should say to him when he came home, and how she certainly never would again let him go out and keep it secret from Nettie. Nettie, for her part, bathed her hot eyes, put on her bonnet, and went out, quietly undoing all the bolts and bars, into the chill morning world, where nobody was yet awake. She was a little uncertain which way to turn, but noway uncertain of her business. Whether he had gone into the town, or towards the low quarter by the banks of the canal, she felt it difficult to conclude. But remembering her own suggestion that he might have stumbled in the field, and fallen asleep there, she took her way across the misty grass. It was still spring, and a little hoar-frost crisped the wintry sod. Everything lay forlorn and chill under the leaden morning skies—not even an early market-cart disturbed the echoes. When the cock crew somewhere, it startled Nettie. She went like a spectre across the misty fields, looking down into the ditches and all the inequalities of the way. On the other side lay the canal, not visible, except by the line of road that wound beside it, from the dead flat around. She bent her steps in that direction, thinking of a certain mean little tavern which, somehow, when she saw it, she had associated with Fred—a place where the men at the door looked slovenly and heated, like Fred himself, and lounged with their hands in their pockets at noon of working-days. Some instinct guided Nettie there.

But she had no need to go so far. Before she reached that place the first sounds of life that she had yet heard attracted Nettie's attention. They came from a boat which lay in the canal, in which the bargemen seemed preparing to start on their day's journey. Some men were leisurely leading forward the horses to the towing-path, while two in the boat were preparing for their start inside. All at once a strange cry rang into the still, chill air—such a cry as startles all who can hear it. The men with the horses hurried forward to the edge of the canal, the bargemen hung over the side of their boat; visible excitement rose among them about something there. Nettie, never afraid, was less timid than ever this morning. Without thinking of the risk of trusting herself with these rude fellows alone, she went straight forward into the midst of them with a curiosity for which she could scarcely account; not anxiety, only a certain wonder and impatience, possessed her to see what they had here.

What had they there?—not a man—a dreadful drowned image, all soiled and swollen—a squalid tragic form, immovable, never to move more. Nettie did not need to look at the dread, uncovered, upturned face. The moment she saw the vague shape of it rising against the side of the boat, a heap of dead limbs, recognisable only as something human, the terrible truth flashed upon Nettie. She had found not him, but It. She saw nothing more for one awful moment—heaven and earth reeling and circling around her, and a horror of darkness on her eyes. Then the cold light opened up again—the group of living creatures against the colourless skies, the dead creature staring and ghastly, with awful dead eyes gazing blank into the shuddering day. The girl steadied herself as she could on the brink of the sluggish current, and collected her thoughts. The conclusion to her search, and answer to all her questions, lay, not to be doubted or questioned, before her. She dared not yield to her own horror, or grief, or dismay. Susan sleeping, unsuspicious, in full trust of his return— the slumbering house into which this dreadful figure must be carried—obliterated all personal impressions from Nettie's mind. She explained to the amazed group who and what the dead man was—where he must be brought to—instantly, silently, before the world was awake. She watched them lay the heavy form upon a board, and took off her own shawl to lay over it, to conceal it from the face of day. Then she went on before them, with her tiny figure in its girlish dress, like a child in the shadow of the rough but pitying group that followed. Nettie did not know why the wind went so chill to her heart after she had taken off her shawl. She did not see the unequal sod under her feet as she went back upon that dread and solemn road. Nothing in the world but what she had to do occupied the throbbing heroic heart. There was nobody else to do it. How could the girl help but execute the work put into her hand? Thinking neither of the hardship nor the horror of such dread work falling to her lot, but only this, that she must do it, Nettie took home to the unconscious sleeping cottage that thing which was Fred Rider; no heavier on his bearers' hands to-day than he had been already for years of his wasted life.

CHAPTER X.

When Nettie opened the door of the sleeping house with the great key she had carried with her in her early dreadful expedition, there was still nobody stirring in the unconscious cottage. She paused at the door, with the four men behind her carrying shoulder-high that terrible motionless burden. Where was she to lay it? In her own room, where she had not slept that night, little Freddy was still sleeping. In another was the widow, overcome by watching and fretful anxiety. The other fatherless creatures lay in the little dressing-room. Nowhere but in the parlour, from which Fred not so very long ago had driven his disgusted brother—the only place she had where Nettie's own feminine niceties could find expression, and where the accessories of her own daily life and work were all accumulated. She lingered even at that dread moment with a pang of natural reluctance to associate that little sanctuary with the horror and misery of this bringing-home; but when every feeling gave way to the pressure of necessity, that superficial one was not like to resist it. Her companions were not aware that she had hesitated even for that moment. She seemed to them to glide softly, steadfastly, without any faltering, before them into the little silent womanly room, where her night's work was folded tidily upon the table, and her tiny thimble and scissors laid beside it. What a heart-rending contrast lay between those domestic traces and that dreadful muffled figure, covered from the light of day with Nettie's shawl, which was now laid down there, Nettie did not pause to think of. She stood still for a moment, gazing at it with a sob of excitement and agitation swelling into her throat; scarcely grief—perhaps that was not possible—but the intensest remorseful pity over the lost life. The rude fellows beside her stood silent, not without a certain pang of tenderness and sympathy in their half-savage hearts. She took her little purse out and emptied it of its few silver coins among them. They trod softly, but their heavy footsteps were heard, notwithstanding, through all the little house. Nettie could already hear the alarmed stirring up-stairs of the master and mistress of the cottage; and, knowing what explanations she must give, and all the dreadful business before her, made haste to get her strange companions away before Mrs Smith came down-stairs. One of them, however, as he followed his comrades out of the room, from some confused instinct of help and pity, asked whether he should not fetch a doctor? The question struck the resolute little girl with a pang sharper than this morning's horror had yet given her. Had she perhaps neglected the first duty of all, the possibility of restoration? She went back, without answering him, to lift the shawl from that dreadful face, and satisfy herself whether she had done, that last irremediable wrong to Fred. As she met the dreadful stare of those dead eyes, all the revulsion of feeling which comes to the hearts of the living in presence of the dead overpowered Nettie. She gave a little cry of inarticulate momentary anguish. The soul of that confused and tremulous outcry was Pardon! pardon! What love was ever so true, what tenderness so constant and unfailing, that did not instinctively utter that cry when the watched life had ended, and pardon could no longer come from those sealed lips? Nettie had not loved that shamed and ruined man—she had done him the offices of affection, and endured and sometimes scorned him. She stood remorseful by his side in that first dread hour, which had changed Fred's shabby presence into something awful; and her generous soul burst forth in that cry of penitence which every human creature owes its brother. The tender-hearted bargeman who had asked leave to fetch a doctor, drew near her with a kindred instinct—"Don't take on, miss—there's the crowner yet—and a deal to look to," said the kind rough fellow, who knew Nettie. The words recalled her to herself—but with the softened feelings of the moment a certain longing for somebody to stand by her in this unlooked-for extremity came over the forlorn courageous creature, who never yet, amid all her labours, had encountered an emergency like this. She laid the shawl reverently back over that dead face, and sent a message to the doctor with lips that trembled in spite of herself. "Tell him what has happened, and say he is to come as soon as he can," said Nettie; "for I do not understand all that has to be done. Tell him I sent you; and now go—please go before they all come down-stairs."

But when Nettie turned in again, after closing the door, into that house so entirely changed in character by the solemn inmate who had entered it, she was confronted by the amazed and troubled apparition of Mrs Smith, half-dressed, and full of wonder and indignation. A gasping exclamation of "Miss!" was all that good woman could utter. She had with her own eyes perceived some of the "roughs" of Carlingford emerging from her respectable door under Nettie's grave supervision, and yet could not in her heart, notwithstanding appearances, think any harm of Nettie; while, at the same time, a hundred alarms for the safety of her household gods shook her soul. Nettie turned towards her steadily, with her face pallid and her brilliant eyes heavy. "Hush," she said; "Susan knows nothing yet. Let her have her rest while she can. We have been watching for him all night, and poor Susan is sleeping, and does not know."

"Know what?—what has happened?—he's been and killed himself? Oh, miss, don't you go for to say so!" cried Mrs Smith, in natural dismay and terror.

"No," cried Nettie, with a long sigh that relieved her breast, "not so bad as that, thank Heaven; but hush, hush! I cannot go and tell Susan just yet—not just yet. Oh, give me a moment to get breath! For he is dead! I tell you, *hush*!" cried Nettie, seizing the woman's hand, and wringing it, in the extremity of her terror for alarming Susan. "Don't you understand me? She is a widow, and she does not know—her husband is dead, and she does not know. Have you no pity for her in your own heart?"

"Lord ha' mercy! but wait till I call Smith," cried the alarmed landlady, shrinking, yet eager to know the horribly interesting details of that tragedy. She ran breathless up-stairs on that errand, while Nettie went back to the door of the parlour, resolutely locked it, and took away the key. "Nobody shall go gazing and talking over him, and making a wonder of poor Fred," said Nettie to herself, shaking off from her long eyelashes the tear which came out of the compunction of her heart. "Poor Fred!" She sat down on one of the chairs of the little hall beside that closed door. The children and their mother up-stairs still slept unsuspicious; and their young guardian, with a world of thoughts rising in her mind, sat still and pondered. The past was suddenly cut off from the future by this dreadful unthought-of event. She had come to a dead pause in that life, which to every spectator was so strangely out of accordance with her youth, but which was to herself such simple and plain necessity as to permit no questioning. She was brought suddenly to a standstill at this terrible moment, and sat turning her dauntless little face to the new trial before her, pale, but undismayed. Nettie did not deceive herself even in her thoughts. She saw, with the intuitive foresight of a keen observer, her sister's violent momentary grief, her indolent acceptance of the position after a while, the selfish reserve of repining and discontent which Susan would establish in the memory of poor Fred: she saw how, with fuller certainty than ever, because now more naturally, she herself, her mind, her laborious hands, her little fortune, would belong to the fatherless family. She did not sigh over the prospect, or falter; but she exercised no self-delusion on the subject. There was nobody but she to do it—nobody but she, in her tender maidenhood, to manage all the vulgar tragical business which must, this very day, confirm to the knowledge of the little surrounding world the event which had happened—nobody but herself to tell the tale to the widow, to bear all the burdens of the time. Nettie did not think over these particulars with self-pity, or wonder over her hard lot. She did not imagine herself to have chosen this lot at all. There was nobody else to do it—that was the simple secret of her strength.

But this interval of forlorn repose was a very brief one. Smith came down putting on his coat, and looking scared and bewildered; his wife, eager, curious, and excited, closely following. Nettie rose when they approached her to forestall their questions.

"My brother-in-law is dead," she said. "He fell into the canal last night and was drowned. I went out to look for him, and—and found him, poor fellow! Oh, don't cry out or make a noise: remember Susan does not know! Now, dear Mrs Smith, I know you are kind—I know you will not vex me just at this moment. I have had him laid *there* till his brother comes. Oh, don't say it's dreadful! Do you think I cannot see how dreadful it is? but we must not think about that, only what has to be done. When Dr Edward comes, I will wake my sister; but just for this moment, oh have patience! I had no place to put him except *there*."

"But, Lord bless us, he mightn't be clean gone: he might be recovered, poor gentleman! Smith can run for Dr Marjoribanks; he is nearer nor Dr Rider," cried the curious excited landlady, with her hand upon the locked door.

Nettie made no answer. She took them into the room in solemn silence, and showed them the stark and ghastly figure, for which all possibilities had been over in the dark midnight waters hours ago. The earliest gleam of sunshine came shining in at that moment through the window which last night Nettie had opened that Fred might see the light in it and be guided home. It seemed to strike like a reproach upon that quick-throbbing impatient heart, which felt as a sin against the dead its own lack of natural grief and affection. She went hurriedly to draw down the blinds and close out the unwelcome light. "Now he is gone, nobody shall slight or scorn him," said Nettie to herself, with hot tears; and she turned the wondering dismayed couple—already awakening out of their first horror, to think of the injury done to their house and "lodgings," and all the notoriety of an inquest—out of the room, and locked the door upon the unwilling owners, whom nothing but her resolute face prevented from bursting forth in selfish but natural lamentations over their own secondary share in so disastrous an event. Nettie sat down again, a silent little sentinel by the closed door, without her shawl, and with her tiny chilled feet on the cold tiles. Nettie sat silent, too much occupied even to ascertain the causes of her personal discomfort. She had indeed enough to think of; and while her little girlish figure, so dainty, so light, so unlike her fortunes, remained in that unusual stillness, her mind and heart were palpitating with thoughts—all kinds of thoughts; not only considerations worthy the solemnity and horror of the moment, but every kind of trivial and secondary necessity, passed through that restless soul, all throbbing with life and action, more self-conscious than usual from the fact of its outward stillness. A hundred rapid conclusions and calculations about the funeral, the mourning, the change of domestic habits involved, darted through Nettie's mind. It was a relief to her to leap forward into these after-matters. The immediate necessity before her—the dreadful errand on which she must presently go to her sister's bedside—the burst of wailing and reproachful grief which all alone Nettie would have to encounter and subdue, were not to be thought of. She bent down her little head into her hands, and once more shed back that hair which, never relieved out of its braids through all this long night, began to droop over her pale cheeks; and a quick sigh of impatience, of energy restrained, of such powerlessness as her courageous capable soul, in the very excess of its courage and capacity, felt in its approaching conflict with the feeble foolish creature, who never could be stimulated out of her own narrow possibilities, burst from Nettie's breast. But the sigh was as much physical as mental—the long-drawn breath of mingled weariness and restlessness—the instinct to be doing, and the exhaustion of long labour and emotion, blended together. Thus she waited while the cold spring morning brightened, and Mrs Smith went about her early domestic business, returning often into the little back-parlour with the mullioned window, of which domestic

Gothic treatment had made a condemned cell, to re-express her anxieties and horrors. Nettie had an instinctive consciousness even of Mrs Smith's grievance. She knew this dismal association would ruin "the lodgings," and felt that here was another bond upon her to remain at St Roque's, however much she might long to escape and flee away.

All these crowding and breathless thoughts were a few minutes after reduced to absolute momentary stillness. It was by a step outside coming hastily with rapid purpose along the silent way. Nettie rose up to meet Edward Rider; not as the angry lover still fiercely resentful of that rejection, which was no rejection, but only a bare and simple statement of necessity; not as the suitor of Miss Marjoribanks; simply as the only creature in the world who could help her, or to whom she would delegate any portion of her own hard but inevitable work. She opened the door before he had time to knock, and held out her hand to him silently, quite unawares betraying her recognition of his step—her comfort in his presence. That meeting flushed the doctor's anxious face with a mingled shame and triumph not expressible in words, but left Nettie as pale, as preoccupied, as much absorbed in her thoughts and duties as before.

"Dr Edward, I should not have sent for you if I could have done it all myself," said Nettie; "but I knew you would think it right to be here now. And I have Susan and the children to look to. I commit this to you."

"Do they know?" said the doctor, taking the key she gave him, and holding fast, with an instinct of compassion almost more strong than love, the little hand which never trembled.

"I will tell Susan, now that you have come—I could not before," said Nettie, with another sigh. "Poor Susan! I was glad to let her sleep."

"But there is no one to think whether you sleep or not," cried Edward Rider. "And those eyes have watched all night. Nettie, Nettie, could not you have sent for me sooner? A word would have brought me at any moment."

"You were not wanted till now," said Nettie, not without a touch of womanly pride. "I have always been able to do my own work, Dr Edward. But, now, don't let us quarrel any more," she said, after a pause. "You were angry once, and I don't wonder. Never mind all that, but let us be friends; and don't let all the people, and strangers, and men who don't belong to us," cried Nettie once more, with hot tears in her eyes, "be hard upon poor Fred!"

The next moment she had vanished up-stairs and left the doctor alone, standing in the little cold hall with the key in his hand, and Mrs Smith's troubled countenance beholding him from far. Edward Rider paused before he entered upon his dismal share of this morning's work. Death itself did not suffice to endear Fred Rider to his brother. But he stood still, with a certain self-reproach, to withdraw his thoughts, if he could, from Nettie, and to subdue the thrill—the most living touch of life—which this meeting had stirred within him, before he entered that miserable chamber of death.

CHAPTER XI.

That dreadful day ebbed over slowly—tedious, yet so full of events and dismal business that it looked like a year rather than a day. The necessary investigations were got through without any special call upon Nettie. She spent the most of the day up-stairs with Susan, whose wild refusal to believe at first, and sullen stupor afterwards, were little different from the picture which Nettie's imagination had already made. The children received the news with wondering stares and questions. That they did not understand it was little, but that they scarcely were interested after the first movement of curiosity, disappointed and wounded the impatient heart, which unconsciously chafed at its own total inability to convey the feelings natural to such a terrible occasion into any bosom but its own. Nettie's perpetual activity had hitherto saved her from this disgust and disappointment. She had been bitterly intolerant by moments of Fred's disgraceful content and satisfaction with his own indulgences, but had never paused to fret over what she could not help, nor contrast her own high youthful humour and sense of duty with the dull insensibility around her. But to-day had rapt the heroic little girl into a different atmosphere from that she had been breathing hitherto. To-day she was aware that her work had been so far taken out of her hands, and acknowledged in her heart that it was best it should be so. She heard the heavy feet of men coming and going, but was not obliged to descend into immediate conflict with all the circumstances of so horrible a crisis. It was a new sensation to Nettie. A year ago, perhaps, she would not have relinquished even that dreadful business to any one;—to-day, the thought of having some one else who did it for her, and took comfort in relieving her burdened hands, fell with singular soothing power upon the heart which had come to a knowledge of its own weakness in these last tedious months; and as Nettie sat upstairs with all the remorseful thoughts of nature in her softened heart, the impossibility of impressing her own emotions upon those around her struck her with a deeper sense of impatience, disappointment, and disgust than ever before. When she went softly into the darkened room where Susan lay in her gloomy bed, divided between wailings over the injuries which poor Fred had suffered, the harshness that had driven him out of doors, and the want of his brother or somebody to take care of him, which had brought the poor fellow to such an end—and complaints of the wrong done to herself, the "want of feeling" shown by her sister, the neglect with which she was treated, Nettie gazed at the sobbing creature with eyes unconsciously wondering, yet but half-surprised. She knew very well beforehand that this was how her dreadful tidings would be received; yet out of her own softened, awed, compunctious heart—her pity too deep for tears over that lost life—Nettie looked with the unbelief of nature at the widowed woman, the creature who had loved him, and been his wife—yet who could only think of somebody else to be blamed, and of herself injured, at that terrible moment when the companion of her life was violently withdrawn from her. And to go out of that obstinately darkened refuge of fretful sorrow, into the room where the blind had been drawn up the moment her back was turned, and where these three tearless children, totally unimpressed by the information which they had received as a piece of news with mingled curiosity and scepticism, occupied themselves with their usual sports, or listened keenly, with sharp remarks, to the sounds below, which only the utmost stretch of Nettie's authority could keep them from descending to investigate, afforded a wonderful reverse to the picture, which startled her in her momentary clearsightedness. The contrast between her own feelings—she who had no bonds of natural affection to Fred, and to whom he had been, by times, a very irksome burden—and theirs, who were his very own, and belonged to him, appeared to Nettie as no such contrast had ever appeared before. *Her* heart alone was heavy with regret over the ruined man—the now for ever unredeemable life: she only, to whom his death was no loss, but even, if she could have permitted that cruel thought to intervene, a gain and relief, recognised with a pang of compassion almost as sharp as grief, that grievous, miserable fate. When, a few minutes after, the noise of the children's play rose to an outburst, Nettie flushed into a momentary effusion of temper, and silenced the heartless imps with a voice and look which they dared not venture to resist. Her rebuke was, however, interrupted by a sudden call from their mother. "How can you have the heart!—Oh, Nettie, Nettie! I knew you had no feeling!—you never had any feeling since you were a baby—but how can you speak so to his poor children, now that he has left them on the cold world?" cried Susan, sobbing, from her bed. If Nettie sprang to her feet in sudden heat and disgust, and peremptorily closed the doors intervening between the children and their mother, nobody will much wonder at that movement of impatience. Perhaps Nettie's eyes had never been so entirely opened to the hopeless character of the charge she had taken upon her, as in the temporary seclusion of that day.

And meanwhile, down-stairs, Edward Rider was superintending all the arrangements of the time for Nettie's sake. Not because it was his brother who lay there, no longer a burden to any man; nor because natural duty pointed him out as the natural guardian of the orphaned family. The doctor, indeed, would have done his duty in such a hard case, however it had been required of him; but the circumstances were different now: the melancholy bustle, the shame, the consciousness that everybody knew what manner of existence this lost life had been, the exposure, the publicity—all that would have wrung with a hundred sharp wounds a spirit so susceptible to public comments—came with dulled force upon the doctor's mind to-day. When the people about saw the grave and seemly composure with which he went about this dismal business, without those starts and flushes of grievous irritation and shame which the very mention of his brother had once brought upon him, they believed, and honoured him in the belief, that death had awakened the ancient fraternal kindness in Edward Rider's heart. But it was not fraternal kindness that smoothed off the rude edges of that burden; it was the consciousness of doing Nettie's work for her, taking her place, sparing that creature, over whom his heart yearned, the hardest and painfulest business she had yet been involved in. We cannot take credit for the doctor which he did not deserve. He forgave Fred when he saw his motionless figure, never more to do evil or offend in this world, laid in pitiful solitude in that room, which still was Nettie's room, and which even in death he grudged to his brother. But Edward's distinct apprehension of right and wrong, and Fred's deserts in this world, were not altered by that diviner compunction which had moved Nettie. He forgave, but did not forget, nor defend with remorseful tenderness his brother's memory. Not for Fred's sake, but Nettie's, he held his place in the troubled cottage, and assumed the position of head of the family. Hard certainties of experience prevented the doctor's unimaginative mind from respecting here the ideal anguish of sudden widowhood and bereavement. This was a conclusion noways unnatural or surprising for such a life as Fred's—and Edward knew, with that contemptuous hardness into which incessant personal contact with the world drives most men, that neither the wife nor the children were capable of deep or permanent feeling. "They will only hang upon *her* all the heavier," he said to himself, bitterly; and for her, with repentant love, Edward Rider exerted himself. In all the house no heart, but Nettie's alone, acknowledged an ache of pity for Fred and his ruined life. "Mrs Rider, to be sure, will feel at first—it's only natural," said Mrs Smith; "but there wasn't nothing else to be looked for; and if it were not hardhearted to say it, and him lying in his coffin, they'll be a deal better off without him nor with him. But Smith and me, we have ourselves to look to, and it's a terrible blow, is this, to a house as was always as respectable as e'er a one in Carlingford. The lodgings is ruined! The very marks of the feet, if it was nothing else!" cried the afflicted landlady, contemplating the scratched tiles in the hall with actual tears of vexation and regret. But this was the true state of the case to every unconcerned spectator. Only Nettie, on whom the burden had fallen, and was yet to fall heaviest, felt the eyes, which were hot and heavy with watching, grow dim with tears of unspeakable compassion. From the fulness of her youth and strength—strength so burdened, youth so dauntless and dutiful—Nettie gazed with a pity too deep for words at the awful spectacle of that existence lost. That the lifeless thing in the room below could have been a man, and yet have come and gone so disastrously through the world, was terrible to think of, to that living labouring creature, in the depth of her own strange toils and responsibilities. Her heart ached over that wretched, miserable fate. Neither toil nor anguish was to be compared to the dread loss of a life sustained by that departed soul.

CHAPTER XII.

In a few days all this solemn crisis was over, and life went on again in its ordinary tame current, closing over the dishonoured grave where Fred found his rest, henceforward nameless in the world that had suffered his existence as a cumberer of the ground for so many years. Had he been the prop of his house and the light of their eyes, life would have gone on again, after that interruption, all the same, with a persistency which nothing can impair. As it was, the diminished household resumed its ordinary course of existence, after a very few days, with little more than outward marks of what had befallen them. It is true that Nettie sat down with a repugnance which she scarcely could either overcome or conceal, to dispense the domestic provisions at the table which shortly before had borne so dread a burden. But nobody thought of that except Nettie; and but for the black dresses and Susan's cap, Fred was as if he had never been.

About a week after the funeral, the doctor went solemnly to visit them in one of those lengthening spring afternoons. Dr Rider was undeniably nervous and excited about this interview. He had been at home under pretence of having luncheon, but in reality to make a solemn toilette, and wind himself up to the courage necessary for a settlement of affairs. As he dashed with agitated haste down Grange Lane, he saw Miss Wodehouse and her sister Lucy coming from St Roque's, where very probably they too had been making a visit of condolence to Nettie; and a little nearer that scene of all his cogitations and troubles appeared, a much less welcome sight, Miss Marjoribanks, whom all Carlingford, a month ago, had declared Dr Rider to be "paying his addresses" to. The guilty doctor took off his hat to that stout and sensible wayfarer, with a pang of self-disgust which avenged Nettie.

Along the very road where that little Titania, eager and rapid, had gone upon her dauntless way so often, to see that comely well-dressed figure, handsome, sprightly, clever—but with such a world of bright youth, tenderness, loveliness, everything that touches the heart of man, between the two! No harm to Miss Marjoribanks; only shame to the doctor, who, out of angry love, pique, and mortification, to vex Nettie, had pretended to transfer the homage due to the fairy princess to that handsome and judicious woman. The experiment had failed as entirely as it deserved to do; and here was Edward Rider, coming back wiser and humbler, content to put that question over again, and stand once more his chance of what his pride had called a rejection, perhaps content to make still greater sacrifices, if the truth were known, and to do anything Nettie asked him, if Nettie would but condescend to ask or enter into terms at all.

He drew up before St Roque's with a dash, which was much more of agitation than display, and, throwing the reins at the head of his little groom, leaped out like a man who did not see where he was going. He saw Mr Wentworth, however, coming out of the church, and turning round amazed to look what vehicle had come to so sudden a standstill there. All the world seemed to be on the road to St Roque's Cottage that spring afternoon. The doctor made a surly gesture of recognition as he passed the curate, who gazed at him in calm astonishment from the church porch. No other intruder appeared between him and the Cottage. He hurried along past the willow-trees with their drooping tassels, surrounded by a certain maze of excitement and agitation. As he went up to the door, it occurred to him suddenly how Nettie had recognised his step that dread morning of Fred's death. The thought came like a stimulus and encouragement to the doctor. He went in with a brighter look, a heart more hopeful. She had opened the door to him before he could knock, held out to him that tiny morsel of a hand which laboured so hard and constantly, said—what did Nettie say? how many times had the doctor conned it over as he went between his patients?—"You were angry once, and, indeed, I don't wonder." The doctor went boldly in under the cordial of these simple words. If she did not wonder that he was angry once, could she think of saying over again that same conclusion which had cast him into such wrathful despair? He went in to try his fortune a second time, secure of his temper at least. *That* could never fail, nor sin against Nettie again.

Edward Rider went in, expectant somehow, even against his reason, to find an altered world in that house from which Fred had gone. He knew better, to be sure, but nature beguiled the young man out of his wisdom. When he went in to the parlour his eyes were opened. Upon the sofa—that same sofa where Fred had lain, all slovenly and mean in his idleness, with his pipe, polluting Nettie's sole retirement—Mrs Fred lay now in her sombre black dress, with the white cap circling her faded face. She had her white handkerchief in her hand, and was carefully arranged upon the sofa, with a chair placed near for sympathisers. At the table, working rapidly as usual, sat Nettie. Sometimes she turned a momentary glance of mingled curiosity and wonder upon her sister. Evidently she did not interfere with this development of sorrow. Nettie had enough to do, besides, with her needlework, and to enjoin a moderate amount of quietness upon Freddy and his little sister, who were building wooden bricks into houses and castles on the floor by her side. When the doctor entered the room he saw how it was with instantaneous insight. Mrs Fred was sitting in state, in the pomp of woe, to receive all the compassionate people who might come to condole with her. Nettie, half impatient, half glad that her sister could amuse herself so, sat in busy toleration, putting up with it, carrying on her own work through it all—and still, as always, those bonds of her own making closed hard and tenacious upon the prop of the house. Even the chance of speaking with her by herself died off into extreme distance. Young Rider, who came in with the full conviction that anger could never more rise in his heart against Nettie, grew pale with passion, resentment, and impatience before he had been a minute in the room. Always the same! Not relieved out of her bondage—closer bound and prisoned than ever! He took, with an impatient involuntary commotion, the chair placed beside the sofa, and sat down in it abruptly with the briefest salutations. His hopes and anticipations all went bitterly back upon his heart. The very rustle of Nettie's arm as she spread out that little black frock upon the table, and put on its melancholy trimmings, exasperated afresh the man who five minutes ago did not believe it possible that he ever could feel an impulse of displeasure against her again.

"I cannot say that I expected to see you, Mr Edward," said Mrs Fred, lifting her handkerchief to her eyes; "indeed, when I remember the last time you were here, I wonder you could think of coming near us. But now my poor dear Fred is gone, we have nobody to protect us—and of course you don't mind how you hurt my feelings. If you had done your duty by my poor fellow when he was living, he might never—never——"

Here Mrs Fred paused, choked by spiteful tears.

"Dr Edward, don't mind what Susan says," said Nettie. "It is very kind of you to come after everything—— If you would only tell the people not to take any notice, but just to let us go on as usual. They all want to be kind, you know—they keep coming, and asking what they can do; and you understand very well there is nothing to do," said Nettie, with a little pride. "We are just as we were before—nothing is changed: one does not like to be unkind, but nobody needs to do anything. We shall get along all the same."

"So it seems, indeed," said Dr Rider, with irrepressible bitterness; "all the same! But, indeed, I came specially to ask what my sister-in-law meant to do," continued the doctor, bent on one last appeal. "Now that you are left to yourself, Mrs Rider, what do you think of doing? Of course you must have some plans about the children and your future life?"

Mrs Fred looked up at him with momentary alarm and dismay. She did not know what the question meant, but a certain vague terror seized her. It seemed to imply somehow that she was now to be left to her own resources. She gave a certain gasp of appeal to "Nettie!" and took refuge once more in her handkerchief. The doctor was desperate—he had no mercy in him.

"Nettie! always Nettie!" cried the young man. "And is it true, Nettie—is it all the same? Are you always to go on toiling for the miserable comforts of other people? What is to become of us? Have you sold yourself to this fate?"

Nettie laid down the little black frock out of her laborious hands. "You have been up all night, Dr Edward," she said, with a certain tenderness, looking at his agitated face; "you are tired out and sick at the heart. I know it makes you say things you would not say; but after all, you know, except poor Fred, whom none of you think of, everything is the very same. I cannot make it different—nothing can make it different. There is Susan plain enough to be seen—and there are the children. Sometimes it has come into my mind," said Nettie, "that as I shall never be able to afford a *very* good education for the children, it would be better to take them out to the colony again, where they might get on better than here. But it is a dreadful long voyage; and we have no near friends there, or anywhere else: and," concluded the steadfast creature, who had dropped these last words from her lips sentence by sentence, as if eager to impress upon her own mind the arguments against that proceeding—"and," said Nettie, with wistful pathetic honesty, not able to deny the real cause of the reluctance altogether, "I don't seem to have the heart for it now."

Dr Rider started up from his chair. He went to Nettie's side with a sudden thrill of agitation and passion. He clasped the hand with which Nettie was smoothing out that little frock, and crushed the delicate fingers in his inconsiderate grasp. "Nettie! if you must carry them always upon your shoulders, cannot we do it together, at least?" cried the doctor, carried away beyond every boundary of sense or prudence. He got down on his knees beside the table, not kneeling to her, but only compelling her attention—demanding to see the answer of her eyes, the quiver of her mouth. For that moment Nettie's defences too fell before this unlooked-for outburst of a love that had forgotten prudence. Her mouth quivered, her eyes filled. If it were possible—if it were only possible!—— They had both forgotten the spectators who gazed with curious eyes, all unaware how deeply their own fate was involved; and that fate was still trembling in the breathless interval, when a vulgar finger touched those delicate balances of possibility, and the crisis was over, perhaps never to return.

"Nettie!" cried Mrs Fred, "if Edward Rider has no respect for me, nor for my poor Fred—my poor, dear, injured husband, that helped to bring him up, and gave up his practice to him, and died, as I might say, by his neglect—Nettie! how can you be so cruel to your sister? How can you go taking his hand, and looking as if he were your lover? You never had any feeling for me, though everybody thinks so much of you. And now I know what I have to expect. The moment my poor dear Fred's head is laid in the grave—as soon as ever you have me in your own hands, and nobody to protect me!—oh, my Fred! my Fred!— as soon as you are gone, this is how they are using your poor helpless family!—and soon, soon I shall die too, and you will not be encumbered with *me*!"

Long before this sobbing speech was concluded, Dr Rider had risen to his feet, and was pacing through the little room with hasty steps of disgust and rage, and an agitation which overwhelmed all his attempts to master it; while Nettie sat supporting her head in her hands, pressing her fingers upon her hot eyes, beholding that fair impossible vision break and disappear from before her. Nettie's heart groaned within her, and beat against the delicate bosom which, in its tender weakness, was mighty as a giant's. She made no answer to her sister's outcry, nor attempted to comfort the hysterical sobbing into which Susan fell. Nettie gave up the hopeless business without being deceived by those selfish demonstrations. She was not even fortunate enough to be able to persuade herself into admiring love and enthusiasm for those to whom necessity obliged her to give up her own life. She said nothing; she knew the sobs would subside, the end would be gained, the insignificant soul lapse into comfort, and with a sigh of compulsory resignation Nettie yielded once more to her fate.

"Dr Edward, do not think of me any more," she said, resolutely, rising and going out to the door with him, in her simplicity and courage. "You see very well it is impossible. I know you see it as well as I do. If we could be friends as we once were, I should be very, very glad, but I don't think it is possible just now. Don't say anything. We both know how it is, and neither of us can help it. If we could get not to think of each other, that would be best," said Nettie, with another sigh; "but in the mean time let us say good-bye, and speak of it no more."

If the doctor did not take his dismissal exactly so—if Nettie's identification of her own sentiments with his did lead to a warmer tenderness in that farewell, which could not be final while such a bond united them, it was at least with an absolute conviction of the impossibility of any closer union that they parted. The doctor sprang into his drag and dashed away to his patients, plunging into the work which he had somewhat neglected during that exciting day. He was not without some comfort as he went about his business with Care behind him, but that very comfort embittered the pang of the compulsory submission. To think he must leave her there with those burdens upon her delicate shoulders—to believe her his, yet not his, the victim of an unnatural bondage—drove Edward Rider desperate as he devoured the way. A hundred times in an hour he made up his mind to hasten back again and snatch her forcibly out of that thraldom, and yet a hundred times had to fall back consuming his heart with fiery irritation, and chafing at all that seemed duty and necessity to Nettie. As he was proceeding on his troubled way it occurred to him to meet—surely everybody in Carlingford was out of doors this particular afternoon!—that prosperous wife, Mrs John Brown, who had once been Bessie Christian. She was a very pale apparition now to the doctor, engrossed as he was with an influence much more imperious and enthralling than hers had ever been; but the sight of her, on this day of all others, was not without its effect upon Edward Rider. Had not she too been burdened with responsibilities which the doctor would not venture to take upon his shoulders, but which another man, more daring, *had* taken, and rendered bearable? As the thought of that possibility occurred to him, a sudden vision of Mrs Fred's faded figure flashed across his eyes. In the excitement of the moment he touched too sharply with his whip that horse which had suffered the penalty of most of his vagaries of temper and imagination for some time past. The long-suffering beast was aggravated out of patience by that unexpected irritation. It was all the doctor could do for the next ten minutes to keep his seat and his command over the exasperated animal, whose sudden frenzy terrified Mrs Brown, and drove her to take refuge in the nearest shop. How little the Carlingford public, who paused at a respectful distance to look on, guessed those emotions which moved the doctor as they watched him subduing his rebellious horse with vigorous arm and passionate looks! Bessie, with a little palpitation at her heart, could not refrain from a passing wonder whether the sight of herself had anything to do with that sudden conflict. Mrs Brown knew little about St Roque's Cottage, but had heard of Miss Marjoribanks, who it was not to be supposed could hold a very absolute sway over the doctor. Meanwhile Dr Rider struggled with his horse with all the intensity of determination with which he would have struggled against his fate had that been practicable. With set teeth and eyes that blazed with sudden rage and resolution, he subdued the unruly brute, and forced it to acknowledge his mastery. When he drove the vanquished animal, all quivering with pain and passion, on its further course, the struggle had refreshed his mind a little. Ah, if life and adverse fortune could but be vanquished so!—but all Edward Rider's resolution and courage died into hopeless disgust before the recollection of Mrs Fred upon that sofa. Even with Nettie at one hand, that peevish

103

phantom on the other, those heartless imps in insolent possession of the wonderful little guardian who would not forsake them, made up a picture which made the doctor's heart sick. No! Nettie was right. It was impossible. Love, patience, charity, after all, are but human qualities, when they have to be held against daily disgusts, irritations, and miseries. The doctor knew as well as Nettie did that he could not bear it. He knew even, as perhaps Nettie did not know, that her own image would suffer from the association; and that a man so faulty and imperfect as himself could not long refrain from resenting upon his wife the dismal restraints of such a burden. With a self-disgust which was most cutting of all, Edward Rider felt that he should descend to that injustice; and that not even Nettie herself would be safe against the effusions of his impatience and indignation. All through the course of this exciting episode in his life, his own foresight and knowledge of himself had been torture to the doctor, and had brought him, in addition to all other trials, silent agonies of self-contempt which nobody could guess. But he could not alter his nature. He went through his day's work very wretched and dejected, yet with an ineffable touch of secret comfort behind all, which sometimes would look him in the face for a moment like a passing sunbeam, yet sometimes seemed to exasperate beyond bearing the tantalising misery of his fate. A more agitated, disturbed, passionate, and self-consuming man than the doctor was not in Carlingford, nor within a hundred miles; yet it was not perfect wretchedness after all.

Nettie, on her part, went back to Mrs Fred in the parlour after she had parted from Edward Rider, with feelings somewhat different from the doctor's. Perhaps she too had indulged a certain pang of expectation as to what might follow after Fred was gone, in the new world that should be after that change; for Nettie, with all her wisdom of experience, was still too young not to believe that circumstances did change everything now and then, even dispositions and hearts. But before Dr Rider knew it—before he had even wound up his courage to the pitch of asking what was now to happen to them—the little Australian had made up her mind to that which was inevitable. The same Susan whose ceaseless discontents and selfish love had driven Nettie across the seas to look for Fred, was now reposing on that sofa in her widow's cap, altogether unchanged, as helpless and unabandonable, as dependent, as much a fool as ever. The superior wretchedness of Fred's presence and life had partially veiled Susan's character since they came to Carlingford. Now she had the field to herself again, and Nettie recognised at once the familiar picture. From the moment when Susan in her mourning came down-stairs, Nettie acknowledged the weakness of circumstances, the pertinacity of nature. What could she do?—she gave up the scarcely-formed germ of hope that had begun to appear in her breast. She made up her mind silently to what must be. No agonies of martyrdom could have made Nettie desert her post and abandon these helpless souls. They could do nothing for themselves, old or young of them; and who was there to do it all? she asked herself, with that perpetual reference to necessity which was Nettie's sole process of reasoning on the subject. Thus considered, the arguments were short and telling, the conclusion unmistakable. Here was this visible piece of business—four helpless creatures to be supported and provided and thrust through life somehow—with nobody in the world but Nettie to do it; to bring them daily bread and hourly tendance, to keep them alive, and shelter their helplessness with refuge and protection. She drew up her tiny Titania figure, and put back her silken flood of hair, and stood upright to the full extent of her little stature, when she recognised the truth. Nobody could share with her that warfare which was hard to flesh and blood. There was nothing to be said on the subject—no possibility of help. She was almost glad when that interview, which she foresaw, was over, and when Edward had recognised as well as herself the necessities of the matter. She went back again out of the little hall where, for one moment and no more, the lights of youth and love had flushed over Nettie, suffusing her paleness with roseblushes. Now it was all over. The romance was ended, the hero gone, and life had begun anew.

"I can't say I ever liked this place," sighed Mrs Fred, when the lamp was lit that evening, and Nettie had come down-stairs again after seeing the children in bed. "It was always dull and dreary to me. If we hadn't been so far out of Carlingford, things might have been very different. My poor Fred! instead of taking care of him, all the dangers that ever could be were put in his way."

This sentence was concluded by some weeping, of which, however, Nettie did not take any notice. Making mourning by lamp-light is hard work, as all poor seamstresses know. Nettie had no tears in the eyes that were fixed intently upon the little coat which was to complete Freddy's outfit; and she did not even look up from that urgent occupation to deprecate Susan's tears.

"I tell you, Nettie, I never could bear this place," said Mrs Fred; "and now, whenever I move, the dreadful thoughts that come into my mind are enough to kill me. You always were strong from a baby, and of course it is not to be expected that you can understand what my feelings are. And Mrs Smith is anything but kind, or indeed civil, sometimes; and I don't think I could live through another of these cold English winters. I am sure I never could keep alive through another winter, now my poor Fred's gone."

"Well?" asked Nettie, with involuntary harshness in her voice.

"I don't care for myself," sobbed Mrs Fred, "but it's dreadful to see you so unfeeling, and to think what would become of his poor children if anything were to happen to me. I do believe you would marry Edward Rider if it were not for me, and go and wrong the poor children, and leave them destitute. Nobody has the feeling for them that a mother has; but if I live another winter in England, I know I shall die."

"You have thought of dying a great many times," said Nettie, "but it has never come to anything. Never mind that just now. What do you want? Do you want me to take you back to the colony all these thousands of miles, after so many expenses as there have been already?—or what is it you want me to do?"

"You always speak of expenses, Nettie: you are very poor-spirited, though people think so much of you," said Susan; "and don't you think it is natural I should wish to go home, now my poor Fred has been taken away from me? And you confessed it would be best for the children. We know scarcely anybody here, and the very sight of *that* Edward that was so cruel to my poor Fred——"

"Susan, don't be a fool," said Nettie; "you know better in your heart. If you will tell me plainly what you want, I shall listen to you; but if not, I will go up-stairs and put away Freddy's things. Only one thing I may tell you at once; you may leave Carlingford if you please, but I shall not. I cannot take you back again to have you ill all the way, and the children threatening to fall overboard twenty times in a day. I did it once, but I will not do it again."

"You *will* not?" cried Susan. "Ah, I know what you mean: I know very well what you mean. You think Edward Rider——"

Nettie rose up and faced her sister with a little gasp of resolution which frightened Mrs Fred. "I don't intend to have anything said about Edward Rider," said Nettie; "he has nothing to do with it one way or another. I tell you what I told him, that I have not the heart to carry you all back again; and I cannot afford it either; and if you want anything more, Susan," added the peremptory creature, flashing forth into something of her old spirit, "I shan't go—and that is surely enough."

With which words Nettie went off like a little sprite to put away Freddy's coat, newly completed, along with the other articles of his wardrobe, at which she had been working all day. In that momentary impulse of decision and self-will a few notes of a song came unawares from Nettie's lip, as she glanced, light and rapid as a fairy, up-stairs. She stopped a minute after with a sigh. Were Nettie's singing days over? She had at least come at last to find her life hard, and to acknowledge that this necessity which was laid upon her was grievous by times to flesh and blood; but not the less for that did she arrange Freddy's little garments daintily in the drawers, and pause, before she went down-stairs again, to cover him up in his little bed.

Susan still sat pondering and crying over the fire. Her tears were a great resource to Mrs Fred. They occupied her when she had nothing else to occupy herself with; and when she cast a weeping glance up from her handkerchief to see Nettie draw her chair again to the table, and lay down a little pile of pinafores and tuckers which required supervision, Susan wept still more, and said it was well to be Nettie, who never was overcome by her feelings. Thus the evening passed dully enough. Just then, perhaps, Nettie was not a very conversable companion. Such interviews as that of this day linger in the heads of the interlocutors, and perhaps produce more notable effects afterwards than at the moment. Nettie was not thinking about it. She was simply going over it again, finding out the tones and meanings which, in the haste and excitement of their occurrence, did not have their full force. The fulness of detail that lingers about such pictures, which are not half apprehended till they have been gone over again and again, is marvellous. The pinafores went unconsciously through Nettie's fingers. She was scarcely aware of Susan crying by the fire. Though it had been in some degree a final and almost hopeless parting, there was comfort behind the cloud to Nettie as well as to the doctor. She had forgotten all about the discussion with which the evening began before Susan spoke again.

"Richard Chatham came home with the last mail," said Susan, making a feeble effort to renew the fight. "He sent me a letter last week, you know. I daresay he will come to see us. Richard Chatham from Melbourne, Nettie. I daresay he will not stay out of the colony long."

Nettie, who was lost in her own thoughts, made no reply.

"I daresay," repeated Mrs Fred, "he will be going out again in a month or two. I do not believe he could bear this dreadful English winter any more than I could. I daresay he'd be glad to take care of us out—if you should change your mind about going, Nettie."

Nettie gave her sister a glance of resolution and impatience—a swift glance upward from her work, enough to show she marked and understood—but still did not speak.

"Richard Chatham was always very good-natured: it would be such a good thing for us to go in the same ship—if you should happen to change your mind about going, Nettie," said Mrs Fred, rising to retire to her room. "I am going to bed to try to get a little sleep. Such wretched nights as I have would kill anybody. I should not wonder if Richard Chatham came some of these days to see us. Poor fellow! he had always a great fancy for *our* family; and it would be *such* a thing for us, Nettie, if you should change your mind about going, to go in the same ship!"

With which Parthian shot Mrs Fred made her way upstairs and retired from the field. Nettie woke with a startled consciousness out of her dreams, to perceive that here was the process of iteration begun which drives the wisest to do the will of fools. She woke up to it for a moment, and, raising her drooping head, watched her sister make her way, with her handkerchief in her hand, and the broad white bands of her cap streaming over her shoulders, to the door. Susan stole a glance round before she disappeared, to catch the startled glance of that resolute little face, only half woke up, but wholly determined. Though Mrs Fred dared not say another word at that moment, she disappeared full of the conviction that her arrow had told, and that the endless persistence with which she herself, a woman and a fool, was gifted, need only be duly exercised to win the day. When Susan was gone, that parting arrow did quiver for a moment in Nettie's heart; but the brave little girl had, for that one night, a protection which her sister wist not of. After the door closed, Nettie fell back once more into that hour of existence which expanded and opened out the more for every new approach which memory made to it. Sweet nature, gentle youth, and the Magician greater than either, came round her in a potent circle and defended Nettie. The woman was better off than the man in this hour of their separation, yet union. He chafed at the consolation which was but visionary; she, perhaps, in that visionary, ineffable solacement found a happiness greater than any reality could ever give.

CHAPTER XIII.

It was some months after the time of this conversation when a man, unlike the usual aspect of man in Carlingford, appeared at the inn with a carpet-bag, and asked his way to St Roque's Cottage. Beards were not common in those days: nobody grew one in Carlingford except Mr Lake, who, in his joint capacity of portrait-painter and drawing-master, represented the erratic and lawless followers of Art to the imagination of the respectable town. But the stranger who made his sudden appearance at the Blue Boar wore such a forest of hair on the lower part of his burly countenance as obliterated all ordinary landmarks in that region, and by comparison made Mr Lake's dainty little mustache and *etceteras* sink into utter propriety and respectableness. The rest of the figure corresponded with this luxuriant feature; the man was large and burly, a trifle too stout for a perfect athlete, but powerful and vigorous almost beyond anything then known in Carlingford. It was now summer, and warm weather, and the dress of the new-comer was as unusual as the other particulars of his appearance. In his broad straw-hat and linen coat he stood cool and large in the shady hall of the Blue Boar, with glimpses of white English linen appearing under his forest of beard, and round his brown sun-scorched wrists. A very small stretch of imagination was necessary to thrust pistols into his belt and a cutlass into his hand, and reveal him as the settler-adventurer of a half-savage disturbed country, equally ready to work or to fight, and more at home in the shifts and expedients of the wilderness than among the bonds of civilisation; yet always retaining, as English adventurers will, certain dainty personal particulars—such, for instance, as that prejudice in favour of clean linen, which only the highest civilisation can cultivate into perfection.

He went off down Grange Lane with the swing and poise of a Hercules when the admiring waiters directed him to the Cottage. Miss Wodehouse, who was standing at the door with Lucy, in the long grey cloak and close bonnet lately adopted by the sisterhood of mercy, which had timidly, under the auspices of the perpetual curate, set itself a-going at St Roque's, looked after the savage man with an instinct of gentle curiosity, wondering where he was going and where he came from. To tell the truth, that tender-hearted soul could with more comfort to herself have stepped down a little on the road to St Roque's, and watched whether that extraordinary figure was in search of Nettie—a suspicion which immediately occurred to her—than she could set out upon the district-visiting, to which Lucy now led her forth. But Miss Wodehouse had tremulously taken example by the late rector, whose abrupt retirement from the duties for which he did not feel himself qualified, the good people in Carlingford had scarcely stopped discussing. Miss Wodehouse, deeply impressed in her gentle mind by the incidents of that time, had considered it her duty to reclaim if possible—she who had no circle of college dons to retire into—her own life from its habits of quiet indolence. She consented to go with Lucy into all the charitable affairs of Carlingford. She stood silent with a pitying face, and believed in all the pretences of beggary which Lucy saw through by natural insight. But it was no more her natural element than the long grey cloak was a natural garment for that spotless, dove-coloured woman. Her eyes turned wistfully after the stranger with suppressed impulses of gentle curiosity and gossip. She knew very well he did not belong to Carlingford. She knew nobody in Grange Lane or the neighbourhood to whom he could belong. She wanted very much to stop and inquire at the stable-boy of the Blue Boar, their own gardener's son, who and what this new-comer was, and turned back to look after him before she turned out of George Street following Lucy, with lively anxiety to know whether he was going to St Roque's. Perhaps the labours of a sisterhood of mercy require a special organisation even of the kind female soul. Miss Wodehouse, the most tender-hearted of human creatures, did not rise to that development; and, with a little pang of unsatisfied wonder, saw the unaccustomed Hercules disappear in the distance without being able to make out whither he was bound.

Nobody, however, who had been privileged to share the advantages of Mrs Fred Rider's conversation for some time back, could be at a loss to guess who this messenger from the wilderness was. It was Richard Chatham come at last—he with whose name Nettie had been bored and punctured through and through from the first day of his introduction into Susan's talk till now. Mrs Fred had used largely in the interval that all-potent torture of the "continual dropping;"—used it so perpetually as, though without producing any visible effect upon Nettie's resolution, to introduce often a certain sickness and disgust with everything into that steadfast soul. Nor did she content herself with her own exertions, but skilfully managed to introduce the idea into the minds of the children—ready, as all children are, for change and novelty. Nettie had led a hard enough life for these three months. She could not meet Edward Rider, nor he her, with a calm pretence of friendship; and Susan, always insolent and spiteful, and now mistress of the position, filled the doctor with an amount of angry irritation which his longings for Nettie's society could not quite subdue. That perpetual barrier between them dismayed both. Meetings which always ended in pain were best avoided, except at those intervals when longing love could not, even under that penalty, refuse itself the gratification; but the dismal life which was lighted up only by those unfrequent, agitating, exasperating encounters, and which flowed on through a hundred petty toilsome duties to the fretful accompaniment of Susan's iterations and the novel persecution now carried on by the children, was naturally irksome to the high-spirited and impatient nature which, now no longer heart-whole or fancy-free, did not find it so easy to carry its own way triumphantly through those heavy clogs of helplessness and folly. In the days when Miss Wodehouse pitied and wondered, Nettie had required no sympathy; she had carried on her course victorious, more entirely conscious of the supreme gratification of having her own way than of the utter self-sacrifice which she made to Fred and his family. But now the time predicted by Miss Wodehouse had arrived. Nettie's own personal happiness had come to be at stake, and had been unhesitatingly given up. But the knowledge of that renunciation dwelt with Nettie. Not all the natural generosity of her mind—not that still stronger argument which she used so often, the mere necessity and inevitableness of the case—could blind her eyes to the fact that she *had* given up her own happiness; and bitter flashes of thought would intervene, notwithstanding even the self-contempt and reproach with which she became aware of them. That doubtful complicated matter, most hard and difficult of mortal problems, pressed hard upon Nettie's mind and heart. In former days, when she scornfully denied it to be self-sacrifice, and laboured on, always indomitable, unconscious that what she did was anything more than the simplest duty and necessity, all was well with the dauntless, all-enterprising soul; but growing knowledge of her own heart, of other hearts, cast dark and perplexing shades upon Nettie, as upon all other wayfarers, in these complex paths. The effect upon her mind was different from the effect to be expected according to modern sentimental ethics. Nettie had never doubted of the true duty, the true necessity, of her position, till she became conscious of her vast sacrifice. Then a hundred doubts appalled her. Was she so entirely *right* as she had supposed? Was it best to relieve the helpless hands of Fred and Susan of their natural duties, and bear these burdens for them, and disable herself, when her time came, from the nobler natural yoke in which her full womanly influence might have told to an extent impossible to it now? These questions made Nettie's head, which knew no fanciful pangs, ache with painful thought, and confused her heart and dimmed her lights when she most needed them to burn brightly. While, at the very time when these doubts assailed her, her sister's repetitions and the rising discontent and agitations of the children, came in to over-cloud the whole business in a mist of sick impatience and disgust. Return to Australia was never out of Susan's mind, never absent from her pertinacious foolish lips. Little Freddy harped upon it all day long, and so did his brother and sister. Nettie said nothing, but retired with exasperated weariness upon her own thoughts—sometimes thinking, tired of the conflict, why not give in to them? why not complete the offering, and remove once for all into the region of impossibility that contradictory longing for another life that still stirred by times in her heart? She had never given expression to this weary inclination to make an end of it, which sometimes assailed her fatigued soul; but this was the condition in which Richard Chatham's visit found her, when that Bushman, breathing of the wilds and the winds, came down the quiet suburban road to St Roque's, and, filling the whole little parlour with his beard and his presence, came stumbling into the confined room, where Mrs Fred still lay on the sofa, and Nettie pursued her endless work.

"Sorry to hear of the poor doctor's accident," said the Australian, to whom Fred bore that title. "But he always was a bit of a rover; though it's sad when it comes to that. And so you are thinking of a return to the old colony? Can't do better, I should say—there ain't room in this blessed old country for anything but tax-gatherers and gossips. I can't find enough air to breathe, for my part—and what there is, is taxed—leastways the light is, which is all the same. Well, Mrs Rider! say the word, ma'am, and I'm at your disposal. I'm not particular for a month or two, so as I get home before next summer; and if you'll only tell me your time, I'll make mine suit, and do the best I can for you all. Miss Nettie's afraid of the voyage, is she? That's a new line for her, I believe. Something taken her fancy in this horrid old box of a place, eh? Ha! ha! but I'll be head-nurse and courier to the party, Miss Nettie, if you trust yourselves to me."

"We don't mean to go back, thank you," said Nettie. "It is only a fancy of Susan's. Nobody ever dreamt of going back. It is much too expensive and troublesome to be done so easily. Now we are here, we mean to stay."

The Bushman looked a little startled, and his lips formed into a whistle of astonishment, which Nettie's resolute little face kept inaudible. "Taken your fancy very much, eh, Miss Nettie?" said the jocular savage, who fancied raillery of one kind or other the proper style of conversation to address to a young lady. Nettie gave that big hero a flashing sudden glance which silenced him. Mr Chatham once more formed an inaudible whew! with his lips, and looked at Mrs Fred.

"But *your* heart inclines to the old colony, Miss Susan?—I beg your pardon—didn't remember what I was saying at that moment. Somehow you look so much as you used to do, barring the cap," said the Australian, "that one forgets all that has happened. You incline to cross the seas again, Mrs Rider, without thinking of the expense?—and very sensible too. There never was a place like this blessed old country for swallowing up a man's money. You'll save as much in a year in the colony as will take you across."

"That is what I always say;—but of course my wishes are little thought of," said Mrs Fred, with a sigh; "of course it's Nettie we have to look to now. If she does not choose, to be sure, it does not matter what I wish. Ah! if I don't look different, I feel different— things are changed *now*."

The Bushman gave a puzzled glance, first at one sister and then at the other. It occurred to him that Fred had not been so much of a strength and protection to his family as this speech implied, and that Nettie had been the person whom Mrs Rider had to "look to" even before they left that colony for which she now sighed. But Mrs Fred, in her sorrow and her white cap, was an interesting figure to the eyes which were not much accustomed to look upon womankind. He had no doubt hers was a hard case. Nettie sat opposite, very busy, silent, and resolute, flashing dangerous sudden glances occasionally at her languid sister and their big visitor. It was confusing to meet those brilliant impatient wrathful eyes; though they were wonderfully bright, they put out the wild man of the woods, and made him feel uncomfortable. He turned with relief to those milder orbs which Mrs Fred buried in her handkerchief. Poor little oppressed woman, dependent upon that little arbitrary sister! The sincerest pity awoke in the Bushman's heart.

"Well!" he said, good-humouredly, "I hope you'll come to be of one mind when Miss Nettie thinks it over again; and you have only to drop me a line to let me know when your plans are formed; and it will go hard with me, but I'll make mine suit them one way or another. All that I can do for you in the way of outfit or securing your passages—or even, if you would allow me——"

Here the good fellow paused, afraid to venture any further. Nettie looked up in a sudden blaze, and transfixed him with her eye.

"We have enough for everything we want, thank you," said Nettie, looking through and through his guilty benevolent intentions, and bringing a flush of confusion to his honest cheeks. "When I say I cannot afford anything, I don't mean to ask anybody's assistance, Mr Chatham. We can do very well by ourselves. If it came to be best for the children—or if Susan keeps on wishing it, and gets her own way, as she generally does," said Nettie, with heightened colour, dropping her eyes, and going on at double speed with her work, "I daresay we shall manage it as we did before. But that is my concern. Nobody in the world has anything to do with it but me."

"Oh, Nettie, dear, you're giving in at last!—do say you'll go! and Mr Chatham promises he'll take care of us on the way," cried Mrs Fred, clasping her hands. They were thin hands, and looked delicate in contrast with her black dress. She was very interesting, pathetic, and tender to the rough eyes of the Bushranger. He thought that imperative little creature opposite, with her brilliant glances, her small head drooping under those heavy braids of hair, her tiny figure and rapid fingers, looked like a little cruel sprite oppressing the melancholy soul. When Nettie rose from the table, goaded into sudden intolerance by that appeal, the climax of the "continual dropping," and threw her work indignantly on the table, and called Freddy to come directly, and get dressed for his walk, the impression made by her supposed arbitrary and imperious behaviour was not diminished. She went out disdainful, making no reply, and left those two to a private conference. Then Mrs Fred unbosomed her bereaved heart to that sympathetic stranger. She told him how different everything was now—how hard it was to be dependent even on one's sister—how far otherwise things might have been, if poor dear Fred had been more prudent: one way or other, all her life through, Susan had been an injured woman. All her desire was to take the children back to the colony before she died. "If Nettie would but yield!" sighed Mrs Fred, clasping her hands.

"Nettie must yield!" cried the Bushranger, full of emotion; and Susan cried a little, and told him how much the poor dear children wished it; and knew in her fool's heart that she had driven Nettie to the extremest bounds of patience, and that a little more persistence and iteration would gain the day.

In the mean time Nettie went out with Freddy—the other two being at school—and took him across the fields for his afternoon walk. The little fellow talked of Australia all the way, with a childish treachery and betrayal of her cause which went to Nettie's heart. She walked by his side, hearing without listening, throbbing all over with secret disgust, impatience, and despair. She too perceived well enough the approaching crisis. She saw that once more all her own resolution—the purpose of her heart—would be overborne by the hopeless pertinacity of the unconvincible, unreasoning fool. She did not call her sister hard names—she recognised the quality without giving it its appropriate title—and recognised also, with a bitterness of resistance, yet a sense of the inevitable, not to be described, the certain issue of the unequal contest. What chance had the generous little heart, the hasty temper, the quick and vivacious spirit, against that unwearying, unreasoning pertinacity? Once more she must arise, and go forth to the end of the world: and the sacrifice must be final now.

CHAPTER XIV.

"Well, it's to be hoped she's going to do well for herself—that's all we've got to do with it, eh? I suppose so," said Mr Wodehouse; "she's nothing to you, is she, but a little girl you've taken a deal of notice of?—more notice than was wanted, if I am any judge. If she does go and marry this fellow from Australia, and he's willing to take the whole bundle back to where they came from, it is the best thing that could happen, in *my* opinion. Sly young dog, that doctor, though, I must say—don't you think so? Well, that's how it appears to me. Let's see; there was Bessie——; hum! perhaps it's as well, in present circumstances, to name no names. There was *her*, in the first instance, you know; and the way he got out of that was beautiful; it was what I call instructive, was that. And then—why then, there was Miss Marjoribanks, you know—capital match that—just the thing for young Rider—set him up for life."

"Papa, pray—*pray* don't talk nonsense," said Miss Wodehouse, with gentle indignation. "Miss Marjoribanks is at least ten years——"

"Oh, stuff!—keep your old-maidish memory to yourself, Molly; who cares for a dozen years or so? Hasn't she all the old Scotchman's practice and his savings?—and a fine woman yet—a fine woman, eh? Well, yes, I think so; and then here's this little wretch of a sister-in-law. Why, the doctor's taken your *rôle*, Wentworth, eh? Well, I suppose what ought to be your *rôle*, you know, though I *have* seen you casting glances at the strange little creature yourself."

"Indeed, I assure you, you are entirely mistaken," said Mr Wentworth, hastily, with a sudden flush of either indignation or guilt. The curate glanced at Lucy Wodehouse, who was walking demurely by his side, but who certainly did prick up her ears at this little bit of news. She saw very well that he had looked at her, but would take no notice of his glance. But Lucy's curiosity was notably quickened, notwithstanding; St Roque's Cottage was wonderfully handy, if the perpetual curate of the pretty suburban church saw anything worth visiting there. Lucy drew up her pretty shoulders in her grey sister-of-mercy cloak, and opened her blue eyes a little wider. She was still in circumstances to defy her reverend lover, if his eyes had declined upon lower attractions than her own. She looked very straight before her with unpitying precision down the road, on which St Roque's Church and Cottage were becoming already visible. The whole party were walking briskly over a path hard with frost, which made their footsteps ring. The air was still with a winterly touch, benumbed with cold, yet every sound rang sharply through that clear cloudless atmosphere, reddened without being warmed by the sun as it approached the west. It was Christmas again, and they were wending their way towards St Roque's to assist at the holiday decorations, for which cartloads of laurel and holly had been already deposited within the church. Lucy Wodehouse was chief directress of these important operations. Her sister had accompanied her, partly to admire Lucy's work, and partly to call at the cottage and see how Nettie was going on. Mr Wodehouse himself had come merely for the pride and pleasure of seeing how much they were indebted to his little girl; and the attendance of the curate was most easily explainable. It was, indeed, astonishing how many extremely necessary and natural "calls of duty" should bring Mr Wentworth's path parallel to that of the Wodehouses. This is why they were all proceeding together on this particular afternoon in the week before Christmas towards St Roque's.

In the church, when the party arrived, a little group of workers were busy. The chancel arch was already bristling with glossy holly-leaves. At a little distance from the active group occupied with this pleasant work, and full of chatter and consultation, as was natural, stood one little figure pointing out to two children the wonders of that decorative art. Every one of the new-comers, except Mr Wodehouse, recognised Nettie before she was aware of their presence. She stood with her bonnet fallen a little back, as it generally was, either by encounter of the wind, or by the quantity and luxuriance of her beautiful hair, looking upwards to the point where she had directed the children's eyes. She looked a little forlorn and solitary, as was natural, all by herself, so near that group of busy girls in the chancel—so little separated from them by age, so entirely divided by circumstances. If a certain softening of half-tender pity shone in the curate's eye, could Lucy Wodehouse blame him? But the fact was, Lucy swept past the little Australian with a very brief salutation, and burst into sudden criticism of the work that had been done in her absence, which startled her collaborateurs, while Mr Wentworth followed her into the chancel with a meekness quite unusual to that young priest. Nettie noted both circumstances with a little surprise; but, not connecting them in the most distant degree with herself, turned round with a little twitch of Freddy's arm to go away, and in doing so almost walked into the arms of her older and more faithful friend. Miss Wodehouse kissed her quite suddenly, touching with her soft old cheek that rounder, fairer, youthful face, which turned, half wondering, half pleased, with the look of a child, to receive her caress. Nettie was as unconscious that Miss Wodehouse's unusual warmth was meant to make up for Lucy's careless greeting, as that Lucy had passed her with a positive flutter of resentment and indignation, and that she had been the subject of the conversation and thoughts of all the party. Miss Wodehouse turned with her, taking Freddy's other hand—a proceeding to which that hero rather demurred. They went out together to the frosty road, where the bare willow-branches rustled between the church and the cottage. When they reached the porch of St Roque's, Nettie instinctively held her breath, and stood still for a moment. Along the footpath in front of them a big figure was passing, and beyond that bearded shadow the doctor's drag flew past with all the separate tones of the horse's feet, the wheels, the jingle of the harness, ringing clear through the sharp unsoftened medium of that frosty atmosphere. The doctor himself had all his attention concentrated upon the windows of the cottage, in which the sun was blazing red. He did not see Nettie in the church porch. He was looking for her too intently in the crimsoned windows, to which he turned his head back as he dashed on. Unawares Nettie clasped the fingers of her little companion tighter in her hand as she watched that unexpected homage. The drag was out of sight in another moment; and in a few seconds more the bell of the cottage pealed audibly, and the door was heard to open, admitting the Bushman, who had come upon one of his frequent visits. That last sound disturbed Nettie's composure, and at the same time brought her back to herself.

"I cannot ask you to go in, for Mr Chatham is there, and Susan of course talking to him," said Nettie, with a quiet breath of restrained impatience, "but I should like to talk to you, please. Let me take the children home, and then I will walk up with you. Mrs Smith is very kind; she will take off their things for them: they behave better now, when I am out for a few minutes—though, to be sure, I never am out much to try them. Come, children; be good, and do not make a great noise till I come back."

"What do you want to talk to *her* for?" asked the little girl, gazing coldly in Miss Wodehouse's face.

"When Nettie went out to tea, we made as much noise as we liked," said Freddy, "but there was papa there. Now there's only mamma, and she's so cross. I hate Chatham—mamma is always crossest when Chatham's there. What do you want to talk to people for, Nettie? Come in, and say there's to be toast, and let us have tea."

"We never have any tea till Nettie comes back," added his sister, looking full once more into Miss Wodehouse's face. The calm childish impertinence disconcerted that gentle woman. She gazed at the wonderful creatures with dumb amazement. Her eyes fell before their steady stare. "I should be sorry to bring you out again, dear, if it's a trouble," began Miss Wodehouse, turning her face with a sense of relief from the hard inspection of the children to their little guardian.

Nettie made no reply, but carried off her children to the cottage door, turned them peremptorily in, and issued her last orders. "If you make a noise, you shall not go," said Nettie; and then came back alert, with her rapid fairy steps, to Miss Wodehouse's side.

"Does not their mother take any charge of them?" faltered the gentle inquisitor. "I never can understand you young people, Nettie. Things were different in my days. Do you think it's quite the best thing to do other people's duties for them, dear? and now I'm so sorry—oh, so sorry—to hear what you are going to do now."

"Susan is delicate," said Nettie. "She never had any health to speak of—I mean, she always got better, you know, but never had any pleasure in it. There must be a great deal in that," continued Nettie, reflectively; "it never comes into my head to think whether I am ill or well; but poor Susan has always had to be thinking of it. Yes, I shall have to take them away," she added again, after a pause. "I am sorry, very sorry too, Miss Wodehouse. I did not think at one time that I had the heart to do it. But on the whole, you know, it seems so much better for them. Susan will be stronger out there, and I have not money enough to give the children a very good education. They will just have to push their way like the others; and in the colony, you know, things are so different. I have no doubt in my own mind now that it will be best for them all."

"But, Nettie, Nettie, what of yourself? will it be best for you?" cried Miss Wodehouse, looking earnestly in her face.

"What is best for them will be best for me," said Nettie, with a little impatient movement of her head. She said so with unfaltering spirit and promptitude. She had come to be impatient of the dreary maze in which she was involved. "If one must break one's heart, it is best to do it at once and have done with it," said Nettie, under her breath.

"What was that you said about your heart?" said Miss

Wodehouse. "Ah, my dear, that is what I wanted to speak of. You are going to be married, Nettie, and I wanted to suggest to you, if you won't be angry. Don't you think you could make some arrangement about your sister and her family, dear?—not to say a word against the Australian gentleman, Nettie, whom, of course, I don't know. A man may be the best of husbands, and yet not be able to put up with a whole family. I have no doubt the children are very nice clever children, but their manner is odd, you know, for such young creatures. You have been sacrificing yourself for them all this time; but remember what I say—if you want to live happily, my dear, you'll have to sacrifice them to your husband. I could not be content without saying as much to you, Nettie. I never was half the good in this world that you are, but I am nearly twice as old—and one does pick up some little hints on the way. That is what you must do, Nettie. Make some arrangement, dear. If he has promised to take them out with you, that is all right enough; but when you come to settle down in your new home, make some arrangement dear."

When Miss Wodehouse arrived breathless at the conclusion of a speech so unusually long for her, she met Nettie's eyes flashing upon her with the utmost surprise and curiosity. "I shall never marry anybody," said Nettie. "What do you mean?"

"Don't say anything so foolish," said Miss Wodehouse, a little nettled. "Do you suppose I don't know and see *that* Mr Chatham coming and going? How often has he been seen since the first time, Nettie? and do you suppose it's all been benevolence? My dear, I know better."

Nettie looked up with a startled glance. She did not blush, nor betray any pleasant consciousness. She cast one dismayed look back towards the cottage, and another at Miss Wodehouse. "Can *that* be why he comes?" said Nettie, with quiet horror. "Indeed, I never thought of it before—but all the same, I shall never marry anybody. Do you imagine," cried the brilliant creature, flashing round upon poor Miss Wodehouse, so as to dazzle and confuse that gentlewoman, "that a man has only to intend such a thing and it's all settled? I think differently. Twenty thousand Chathams would not move me. I shall never marry anybody, if I live to be as old as—as you, or Methuselah, or anybody. It is not my lot. I shall take the children out to Australia, and do the best I can for them. Three children want a great deal of looking after—and after a while in Carlingford, you will all forget that there ever was such a creature as Nettie. No, I am not crying. I never cry. I should scorn to cry about it. It is simply *my business*. That is what it is. One is sorry, of course, and now and then it feels hard, and all that. But what did one come into the world for, I should like to know? Does anybody suppose it was just to be comfortable, and have one's own way? I have had my own way a great deal—more than most people. If I get crossed in some things, I have to bear it. That is all I am going to say. I have got other things to do, Miss Wodehouse. I shall never marry anybody all my life."

"My dear, if you are thrown upon this Mr Chatham for society all the time of the voyage, and have nobody else to talk to——" said the prudent interlocutor.

"Then we'll go in another ship," cried Nettie, promptly; "that is easily managed. I know what it is, a long voyage with three children—they fall up the cabin-stairs, and they fall down the forecastle; and they give you twenty frights in a day that they will drop overboard. One does not have much leisure for anything— not even for thinking, which is a comfort sometimes," added Nettie, confidentially, to herself.

"It depends upon what you think of, whether thinking is a comfort or not," said good Miss Wodehouse. "When I think of you young people, and all the perplexities you get into! There is Lucy now, vexed with Mr Wentworth about something—oh, nothing worth mentioning; and there was poor Dr Rider! How he did look behind him, to be sure, as he went past St Roque's! I daresay it was you he was looking for, Nettie. I wish you and he could have fancied each other, and come to some arrangement about poor Mr Fred's family—to give them so much to live on, or something. I assure you, when I begin to think over such things, and how perverse both people and circumstances are, thinking is very little comfort to me."

Miss Wodehouse drew a long sigh, and was by no means disinclined to cry over her little companion. Though she was the taller of the two, she leant upon Nettie's firm little fairy arm as they went up the quiet road. Already the rapid winter twilight had fallen, and before them, in the distance, glimmered the lights of Carlingford—foremost among which shone conspicuous the large placid white lamp (for professional reds and blues were beneath his dignity) which mounted guard at Dr Marjoribanks's garden gate. Those lights, beginning to shine through the evening darkness, gave a wonderful look of home to the place. Instinctively there occurred to Nettie's mind a vision of how it would be on the sea, with a wide dark ocean heaving around the solitary speck on its breast. It did not matter! If a silent sob arose in her heart, it found no utterance. Might not Edward Rider have made that suggestion which had occurred only to Miss Wodehouse? Why did it never come into his head that Susan and her family might have a provision supplied for them, which would relieve Nettie? He had not thought of it, that was all. Instead of that, he had accepted the impossibility. Nettie's heart had grown impatient in the maze of might-be's. She turned her back upon the lights, and clasped Miss Wodehouse's hand, and said good-night hastily. She went on by herself very rapidly along the hard gleaming road. She did not pay any attention to her friend's protestation that she too was coming back again to St Roque's to join Lucy—on the contrary, Nettie peremptorily left Miss Wodehouse, shaking hands with her in so resolute a manner that her gentle adviser felt somehow a kind of necessity upon her to pursue her way home; and, only when Nettie was nearly out of sight, turned again with hesitation to retrace her steps towards St Roque's. Nettie, meanwhile, went on at a pace which Miss Wodehouse could not possibly have kept up with, clasping her tiny hands together with a swell of scorn and disdain unusual to it in her heart. Yes! Why did not Edward Rider propose the "arrangement" which appeared feasible enough to Miss Wodehouse? Supposing even Nettie had refused to consent to it, as she might very probably have done with indignation—still, why did it not occur to Dr Edward? She asked herself the question with a heat and passion which she found it difficult to account for. She half despised her lover, as woman will, for obeying her—almost scorned him, as woman will, for the mere constancy which took no violent measures, but only suffered and accepted the inevitable. To submit to what cannot be helped is a woman's part. Nettie, hastening along that familiar path, blazed into a sudden burst of rage against Edward because he submitted. What he could do else she was as ignorant of as any unreasonable creature could be. But that mattered little. With indignation she saw herself standing on the verge of that domestic precipice, and the doctor looking on, seeing her glide out of his reach, yet putting forth no violent sudden hand to detain her. All the impatience of her fiery nature boiled in her veins as she hasted to the cottage, where Susan was discussing their journey with her Australian visitor. No remnant of pathos or love-sickening remained about Nettie, as she flashed in upon them in all her old haste and self-reliance—resolute to precipitate the catastrophe which nobody took any measures to prevent.

CHAPTER XV.

It was not long before the doctor was made aware of the ghost in his troubled path. Nobody in Carlingford could meet the big Bushman in those streets, which always looked too narrow for him, without a certain curiosity about that savageman. Dr Rider had observed him with jealous interest on his very first appearance, but had hitherto connected no idea but that of a return to Australia, which he felt sure Nettie would never consent to, with the big stranger. With such a thought he had seen him making his way towards the cottage that very evening when he himself turned back, as long as those crimsoned windows were visible, to look for Nettie, who did not show herself. The doctor was bound to see a distant patient, miles on the other side of Carlingford. As he dashed along over the echoing road he had time to imagine to himself how Nettie might at that very moment be badgered and persecuted; and when he had seen his patient and done his duty, and with the lamps lighted in the drag, and the frosty wind blowing keen on his face, and the lights of Carlingford cheering him on in the distance, was once more returning, an impatience, somewhat akin to Nettie's, suddenly came upon the doctor. Akin, yet different; for in his case it was an impulse of sensation, an inspiration of the exhilarating speed and energy of motion with which he flew through the bracing air, master of himself, his horse, and the long sweep of solitary road before him. Again it occurred to Dr Rider to dash forward to St Roque's and carry off Nettie, oppose it who would. The idea pleased him as he swept along in the darkness, its very impossibility making the vision sweeter. To carry her off at a stroke, in glorious defiance of circumstances, and win happiness and love, whatever might ensue. In the flush of the moment the doctor suddenly asked himself whether this, after all, were not the wisest course? whether, whatever might come of it, happiness was not worth the encounter of the dark array of troubles behind? and whether to precipitate everything by a sudden conclusion might not be the best way of solving all the intricacies of the matter? He was still in this mood when he arrived at his own house, where dinner, as usual, was not improved by having been ready for an hour. The lamp was not lighted when he came in, and only the cold reflection of the street lights outside, with a particoloured gleam at the corner window from his own red and blue professional ensign at the surgery door, lighted the solitary little room, where he looked in vain even for so much as a note or letter to bring some shadow of human fellowship to his home; the fire smouldering dully, the big chair turned with a sullen back against the wall, as if nobody ever sat there—though Nettie had once and for ever appropriated it to her use—everything in such inhuman trim and good order disgusted the doctor. He rang his bell violently for the lights and refreshments which were so slow of coming, and, throwing himself into that chair, bit his nails and stared out at the lamplight in the rapid access of thought that came upon him. The first thing that disturbed him in this was the apparition of a figure outside peering in with some anxiety at the blank windows—somebody who was evidently curious to know whether the doctor had yet come home. The unhappy doctor started, and rang his bell once more with furious iteration. He knew what was coming. Somebody else, no doubt, had taken ill, without any consideration for young Rider's dinner, which, however, a man must manage to swallow even when tormented with importunate patients, and in love. But the knock of the untimely visitor sounded at the much-assailed door before Mary, sulky and resistant, had been able to arrange before the hungry doctor the half-warm half-cold viands which his impatience would not permit to be duly "heated up;" and he had just seated himself to dispose of the unsatisfactory meal when the little groom, who was as tired as his master, opened the door for Mrs Smith from St Roque's. Mrs Smith was a familiar periodical visitor at Dr Rider's. She had not ceased to hold to that hasty and unwise financial arrangement into which the doctor was persuaded to enter when Fred's pipe had exasperated the landlady into rebellion. He had supplemented the rent at that exciting moment rather than have Nettie disturbed; and now that poor Fred's pipe was extinguished for ever, the doctor still paid the imposition demanded from him—half because he had no time to contest it, half because it was, however improper and unnecessary, a kind of pleasure to do something for Nettie, little as she knew and deeply as she would have resented it. Dr Rider's brows cleared up at sight of Nettie's landlady. He expected some little private anecdotes of her and her ways, such as no one else could give him. He gave Mrs Smith a chair with a benignity to which she had no personal claim. Her arrival made Dr Rider's beefsteak palatable, though the cookery and condition of the same were, to say the least, far from perfect. Mrs Smith evidently was a little embarrassed with the gracious reception she received. She twisted the corner of her shawl in her fingers as if it had been that apron with which women of her class habitually relieve their feelings. She was in a false position. She came with the worst of news to the melancholy lover, and he treated her as if she brought some special message or favour from the lady of his thoughts.

"Well, Mrs Smith, and how are you all at the cottage?" said the doctor, applying himself leisurely to his beefsteak.

"Well, doctor, nothing to brag of," said Mrs Smith, fixing her eyes upon the fringe of her shawl. "I haven't nothing to say that's pleasant, more the pity. I don' know, sir, how you'll take it when you come to hear; but it's come very hard upon me. Not for the sake of the lodgings, as'll let again fast enough, now the poor gentleman's sad fate is partly forgotten; but you know, doctor, a body gets attached-like when one set of people stays long enough to feel at home; and there ain't many young ladies like Miss if you were to search the country through. But, now she's really give in to it herself, there ain't no more to be said. I never could bring myself to think Miss would give in till to-night when she told me; though Smith he always said, when the stranger gentleman took to coming so constant, as he knew how it would be."

"For heaven's sake, what do you mean?" cried Dr Rider, pushing away his plate, and rising hurriedly from that dinner which was fated never to be eaten. Mrs Smith shook her head and drew out her handkerchief.

"I know nothing more, doctor, but just they're going off to Australia," said the landlady, mournfully; "and Miss has started packing the big boxes as have been in the hattic since ever they come: they're going off back where they come from—that's all as I know."

"Impossible!" cried the doctor.

"I'd have said so myself this morning," said Mrs Smith; "but there ain't nothing impossible, doctor, as Miss takes in her head. Don't you go and rush out after her, Dr Rider. I beg of you upon my knees, if it was my last word! I said to Smith I'd come up and tell the doctor, that he mightn't hear from nobody promiscuous as couldn't explain, and mightn't come rushing down to the cottage to know the rights of it and find the gentleman there unexpected. If there's one thing I'm afeard of, it's a quarrel between gentlemen in my house. So, doctor, for the love of peace, don't you go anear the cottage. I'll tell you everything if you listen to me."

The doctor, who had snatched up his hat and made a rapid step towards the door, came back and seized hold of his visitor's shoulder, all his benignity having been put to flight by her unlooked-for revelation. "Look here! I want the truth, and no gossip! What do you mean—what gentleman? What is it all about?" cried Dr Rider, hoarse with sudden passion.

"Oh, bless you, doctor, don't blame it upon me, sir," cried Mrs Smith. "It ain't neither my fault nor my business, but that you've always been kind, and my heart warms to Miss. It's the gentleman from Australia as has come and come again; and being an unmarried gentleman, and Miss—you know what she is, sir—and I ask you, candid, Dr Rider, what was anybody to suppose?"

The doctor grew wildly red up to his hair. He bit his lips over some furious words which Carlingford would have been horrified to hear, and grasped Mrs Smith's shoulder with a closer pressure. "What did she tell you?" said the doctor. "Let me have it word for word. Did she say she was going away?—did she speak of this—this—fellow?" exclaimed the doctor, with an adjective over which charity drops a tear. "Can't you tell me without any supposes, what did she say?"

"I'm not the woman to stand being shook—let me go this minute, sir," cried Mrs Smith. "The Australian gentleman is a very nice-spoken civil man, as was always very respectful to me. She came into my back-parlour, doctor, if you will know so particular—all shining and flashing, like as she does when something's happened. I don't make no doubt they had been settling matters, them two, and so I told Smith. 'Mrs Smith,' said Miss, in her hasty way, enough to catch your breath coming all of a sudden, 'I can't stand this no longer—I shall have to go away—it ain't no good resisting.' Them were her very words, Dr Rider. 'Get me out the big boxes, please,' said Miss. 'It's best done quietly. You must take your week's notice, Mrs Smith, from this day;' and with that she kept moving about the room all in a flutter like, not able to rest. 'Do go and get me out those boxes; there's always a ship on the 24th,' she says, taking up my knitting and falling to work at it to keep her hands steady. 'The day afore Christmas!' says I; 'and oh, Miss, it's running in the face of Providence to sail at this time of the year. You'll have dreadful weather, as sure as life.' You should have seen her, doctor! She gave a sort of smile up at me, all flashing as if those eyes of her were the sides of a lantern, and the light bursting out both there and all over. 'All the better,' she says, as if she'd have liked to fight the very wind and sea, and have her own way even there. Bless you, she's dreadful for having her own way. A good easy gentleman now, as didn't mind much—Dr Rider—Doctor!—you're not agoing, after all I've told you? Doctor, doctor, I say——"

But what Mrs Smith said was inaudible to Edward Rider. The door rang in her ears as he dashed it after him, leaving her mistress of the field. There, where he had once left Nettie, he now, all-forgetful of his usual fastidious dislike of gossip, left Mrs Smith sole occupant of his most private territories. At this unlooked-for crisis the doctor had neither a word nor a moment to spend on any one. He rushed out of the house, oblivious of all those professional necessities which limit the comings and goings of a doctor in great practice; he did not even know what he was going to do. Perhaps it was an anxious husband or father whom he all but upset as he came out, with sudden impetuosity, into the unfrequented street; but he did not stop to see. Pale and desperate, he faced the cold wind which rushed up between the blank garden-walls of Grange Lane. At Mr Wodehouse's door he stumbled against young Wentworth coming out, and passed him with a muttered exclamation which startled the curate. All the floating momentary jealousies of the past rushed back upon the doctor's mind as he passed that tall figure in the wintry road: how he had snatched Nettie from the vague kindnesses of the young clergyman—the words he had addressed to her on this very road—the answer she had given him once, which had driven him wild with passion and resentment. Impossible! the Australian, it appeared, had found nothing impossible in those circumstances in which Nettie had intrenched herself. Had the doctor's wisdom been monstrous folly, and his prudence the blindest shortsightedness? He asked himself the question as he rushed on towards that lighted window shining far along the dark road—the same window which he had seen Nettie's shadow cross, which had been opened to light poor Fred upon the way he never could tread again. Within that jealous blind, shining in that softened domestic light, what drama, murderous to the doctor's peace, might be going on now?

CHAPTER XVI.

Nettie had taken her resolution all at once. Breathless in sudden conviction, angry, heated, yet seeing in the midst of her excitement no help but an immediate action, the hasty little woman had darted into the heart of the difficulty at once. Every moment she lingered wore her out and disgusted her more with the life and fate which, nevertheless, it was impossible to abandon or shrink from. Nothing was so safe as to make matters irrevocable—to plunge over the verge at once. All gleaming with resolve and animation—with the frosty, chill, exhilarating air which had kindled the colour in her cheeks and the light in her eyes—with haste, resentment, every feeling that can quicken the heart and make the pulses leap—Nettie had flashed into the little parlour, where all was so quiet and leisurely. There Susan sat in close confabulation with the Bushman. The children had been banished out of the room, because their mother's head was not equal to their noise and restlessness. When they came in with Nettie, as was inevitable, Mrs Fred sustained the invasion with fretful looks and a certain peevish abstraction. She was evidently interrupted by the rapid entrance, which was as unwelcome as it was hasty. Cold though the night was, Mrs Fred, leaning back upon her sofa, fanned her pink cheeks with her handkerchief, and looked annoyed as well as disturbed when her children came trooping into the room clamorous for tea behind the little impetuous figure which at once hushed and protected them. Susan became silent all at once, sank back on the sofa, and concealed the faded flush upon her cheeks and the embarrassed conscious air she wore behind the handkerchief which she used so assiduously. Neither she nor her visitor took much share in the conversation that rose round the domestic table. Nettie,

135

too, was sufficiently absorbed in her own concerns to say little, and nobody there was sufficiently observant to remark what a sudden breath of haste and nervous decision inspired the little household ruler as she dispensed the family bread-and-butter. When tea was over, Nettie sent her children out of the way with peremptory distinctness, and stayed behind them to make her communication. If she noticed vaguely a certain confused impatience and desire to get rid of her in the looks of her sister and the Australian, she attached no distinct meaning to it, but spoke out with all the simplicity of an independent power, knowing all authority and executive force to lie in her own hands alone.

"When do you think you can be ready to start? My mind is made up. I shall set to work immediately to prepare," said Nettie. "Now, look here, Susan: you have been thinking of it for months, so it is not like taking you by surprise. There is a ship that sails on the 24th. If everything is packed and ready, will you consent to go on that day?"

Mrs Fred started with unfeigned surprise, and, not without a little consternation, turned her eyes towards her friend before answering her sister. "It is just Nettie's way," cried Susan—"just how she always does—holds out against you to the very last, and then turns round and darts off before you can draw your breath. The 24th! and this is the 19th! Of course we can't do it, Nettie. I shall want quantities of things, and Mr Chatham, you know, is not used to your ways, and can't be whisked off in a moment whenever you please."

"I daresay it's very kind of Mr Chatham," said Nettie; "but I can take you out very well by myself—just as well as I brought you here. And I can't afford to get you quantities of things, Susan. So please to understand I am going off to pack up, and on the 24th we shall go."

Once more, under Nettie's impatient eyes, a look and a smile passed between her sister and the Australian. Never very patient at any time, the girl was entirely aggravated out of all toleration now.

"I can't tell what you may have to smile to each other about," said Nettie. "It is no very smiling business to me. But since I am driven to it, I shall go at once or not at all. And so that you understand me, that is all I want to say."

With which words she disappeared suddenly to the multitudinous work that lay before her, thinking as little of Susan's opposition as of the clamour raised by the children, when the hard sentence of going half an hour earlier to bed was pronounced upon them. Nettie's haste and peremptoriness were mixed, if it must be told, with a little resentment against the world in general. She had ceased being sad—she was roused and indignant. By the time she had subdued the refractory children, and disposed of them for the night, those vast Australian boxes, which they had brought with them across the seas, were placed in the little hall, under the pale light of the lamp, ready for the process of packing, into which Nettie plunged without a moment's interval. While Mrs Smith told Edward Rider her story, Nettie was flying up and down stairs with armfuls of things to be packed, and pressing Smith himself into her service. Ere long the hall was piled with heaps of personal property, ready to be transferred to those big receptacles. In the excitement of the work her spirit rose. The headlong haste with which she carried on her operations kept her mind in balance. Once or twice Susan peeped out from the parlour door, and something like an echo of laughter rang out into the hall after one of those inspections. Nettie took no notice either of the look or the laugh. She built in those piles of baggage with the rapidest symmetrical arrangement, to the admiration of Smith, who stood wondering by, and did what he could to help her, with troubled good-nature. She did not stop to make any sentimental reflections, or to think of the thankless office in which she was about to confirm herself beyond remedy by this sudden and precipitate step. Thinking had done Nettie little good hitherto. She felt herself on her true ground again, when she took to doing instead. The lamp burned dimly overhead, throwing down a light confused with frost upon the hall, all encumbered with the goods of the wandering family. Perhaps it was with a certain unconscious symbolism that Nettie buried her own personal wardrobe deep in the lowest depths, making that the foundation for all the after superstructure. Smith stood by, ready to hand her anything she might want, gazing at her with doubtful amazement. The idea of setting off to Australia at a few days' notice filled him with respect and admiration.

"A matter of a three months' voyage," said Smith; "and if I might make bold to ask, Miss, if the weather ain't too bad for anything, how will you pass away the time on board ship when there ain't nobody to speak to?—but, to be sure, the gentleman——"

"The gentleman is not going with us," said Nettie, peremptorily—"and there are the children to pass away the time. My time passes too quick, whatever other people's may do. Where is Mrs Smith, that I see nothing of her to-night? Gone out!—how very odd she should go out now, of all times in the world. Where has she gone, do you suppose? Not to be ungrateful to you, who are very kind, a woman is, of course, twenty times the use a man is, in most things. Thank you—not that; those coloured frocks now—there! that bundle with the pink and the blue. One would suppose that even a man might know coloured frocks when he saw them," said Nettie, with despairing resignation, springing up from her knees to seize what she wanted. "Thank you—I think, perhaps, if you would just go and make yourself comfortable, and read your paper, I should get on better. I am not used to having anybody to help me. I got on quite as well, thank you, by myself."

Smith withdrew, not without some confusion and discomfort, to his condemned cell, and Nettie went on silent and swift with her labours. "Quite as well! better!" said Nettie to herself. "Other people never will understand. Now, I know better than to try anybody." If that hasty breath was a sigh, there was little sound of sorrow in it. It was a little gust of impatience, indignation, intolerance even, and hasty self-assertion. She alone knew what she could do, and must do. Not one other soul in the world beside could enter into her inevitable work and way.

Nettie did not hear the footstep which she might have recognised ringing rapidly down the frosty road. She was too busy rustling about with perpetual motion, folding and refolding, and smoothing into miraculous compactness all the heterogeneous elements of that mass. When a sudden knock came to the door she started, struck with alarm, then paused a moment, looking round her, and perceiving at one hasty glance that nobody could possibly enter without seeing both herself and her occupation, made one prompt step to the door, which nobody appeared to open. It was Mrs Smith, no doubt; but the sudden breathless flutter which came upon Nettie cast doubts upon that rapid conclusion. She opened it quickly, with a certain breathless, sudden promptitude, and looked out pale and dauntless, understanding by instinct that some new trial to her fortitude was there. On the other hand, Edward Rider pressed in suddenly, almost without perceiving it was Nettie. They were both standing in the hall together, before they fully recognised each other. Then the doctor, gazing round him at the unusual confusion, gave an involuntary groan out of the depths of his heart. "Then it is true!" said Dr Rider. He stood among the chaos, and saw all his own dreams broken up and shattered in pieces. Even passion failed him in that first bitterness of conviction. Nettie stood opposite, with the sleeves of her black dress turned up from her little white nimble wrists, her hair pushed back from her cheeks, pushed quite behind one delicate ear, her eyes shining with all those lights of energy and purpose which came to them as soon as she took up her own character again. She met his eye with a little air of defiance, involuntary, and almost unconscious. "It is quite true," said Nettie, bursting forth in sudden self-justification; "I have my work to do, and I must do it as best I can. I cannot keep considering you all, and losing my life. I must do what God has given me to do, or I must die."

Never had Nettie been so near breaking down, and falling

into sudden womanish tears and despair. She would not yield to the overpowering momentary passion. She clutched at the bundle of frocks again, and made room for them spasmodically in the box which she had already packed. Edward Rider stood silent, gazing at her as in her sudden anguish Nettie pulled down and reconstructed that curious honeycomb. But he had not come here merely to gaze, while the catastrophe was preparing. He went up and seized her busy hands, raised her up in spite of her resistance, and thrust away, with an exclamation of disgust, that great box in which all his hopes were being packed away. "There is first a question to settle between you and me," cried the doctor: "you shall not do it. No; I forbid it, Nettie. Because you are wilful," cried Edward Rider, hoarse and violent, grasping the hands tighter, with a strain in which other passions than love mingled, "am I to give up all the rights of a man? You are going away without even giving me just warning—without a word, without a sign; and you think I will permit it, Nettie? Never—by heaven!"

"Dr Edward," said Nettie, trembling, half with terror, half with resolution, "you have no authority over me. We are two people—we are not one. I should not have gone away without a word or a sign. I should have said good-bye to you, whatever had happened; but that is different from permitting or forbidding. Let us say good-bye now and get it over, if that will please you better," she cried, drawing her hands from his grasp; "but I do not interfere with your business, and I must do mine my own way."

The doctor was in no mood to argue. He thrust the big box she had packed away into a corner, and closed it with a vindictive clang. It gave him a little room to move in that little commonplace hall, with its dim lamp, which had witnessed so many of the most memorable scenes of his life. "Look here," cried Dr Rider; "authority has little to do with it. If you had been my wife, Nettie, to be sure you could not have deserted me. It is as great a cruelty—it is as hard upon me, this you are trying to do.

I have submitted hitherto, and heaven knows it has been bitter enough; and you scorn me for my submission," said the doctor, making the discovery by instinct. "When a fellow obeys you, it is only contempt you feel for him; but I tell you, Nettie, I will bear it no longer. You shall not go away. This is not to be. I will neither say good-bye, nor think of it. What is your business is my business; and I declare to you, you shall not go unless I go too. Ah—I forgot. They tell me there is a fellow, an Australian, who ventures to pretend—I don't mean to say I believe it. You think *he* will not object to your burdens! Nettie! Don't let us kill each other. Let us take all the world on our shoulders," cried the doctor, drawing near again, with passionate looks, "rather than part!"

There was a pause—neither of them could speak at that moment. Nettie, who felt her resolution going, her heart melting, yet knew she dared not give way, clasped her hands tight in each other and stood trembling, yet refusing to tremble; collecting her voice and thoughts. The doctor occupied that moment of suspense in a way which might have looked ludicrous in other circumstances, but was a relief to the passion that possessed him. He dragged the other vast Australian box to the same corner where he had set the first, and piled them one above the other. Then he collected with awkward care all the heaps of garments which lay about, and carried them off in the other direction to the stairs, where he laid them carefully with a clumsy tenderness. When he had swept away all these encumbrances, as by a sudden gust of wind, he came back to Nettie, and once more clasped the firm hands which held each other fast. She broke away from him with a sudden cry—

"You acknowledged it was impossible!" cried Nettie. "It is not my doing, or anybody's; no one shall take the world on his shoulders for my sake—I ask nobody to bear my burdens. Thank you for not believing it—that is a comfort at least. Never, surely, any one else—and not you, not you! Dr Edward, let us make an end of it. I will never consent to put my yoke upon your shoulders, but I—I will never forget you or blame you—any more. It is all hard, but we cannot help it. Good-bye—don't make it harder, you, who are the only one that——; good-bye,—no more—don't say any more."

At this moment the parlour door opened suddenly; Nettie's trembling mouth and frame, and the wild protest and contradiction which were bursting from the lips of the doctor, were lost upon the spectator absorbed in her own affairs, and full of excitement on her own account, who looked out. "Perhaps Mr Edward will walk in," said Mrs Fred. "Now he is here to witness what I mean, I should like to speak to you, please, Nettie. I did not think I should ever appeal to you, Mr Edward, against Nettie's wilfulness—but, really now, we, none of us, can put up with it any longer. Please to walk in and hear what I've got to say."

The big Bushman stood before the little fire in the parlour, extinguishing its tiny glow with his vast shadow. The lamp burned dimly upon the table. A certain air of confusion was in the room. Perhaps it was because Nettie had already swept her own particular belongings out of that apartment, which once, to the doctor's eyes, had breathed of her presence in every corner— but it did not look like Nettie's parlour to-night. Mrs Fred, with the broad white bands of her cap streaming over her black dress, had just assumed her place on the sofa, which was her domestic throne. Nettie, much startled and taken by surprise, stood by the table, waiting with a certain air of wondering impatience what was to be said to her—with still the sleeves turned up from her tiny wrists, and her fingers unconsciously busy expressing her restless intolerance of this delay by a hundred involuntary tricks and movements. The doctor stood close by her, looking only at Nettie, watching her with eyes intent as if she might suddenly disappear from under his very gaze. As for the Australian, he stood uneasy under Nettie's rapid investigating glance, and the slower survey which Dr Rider made on entering. He plucked at his big beard, and spread out his large person with a confusion and embarrassment rather more than merely belonged to the stranger in a family party; while Mrs Fred, upon her sofa, took up her handkerchief and once more began to fan her pink cheeks. What was coming? After a moment's pause, upon which Nettie could scarcely keep herself from breaking, Susan spoke.

"Nettie has always had the upper hand so much that she thinks I am always to do exactly as she pleases," burst forth Mrs Fred; "and I don't doubt poor Fred encouraged her in it, because he felt he was obliged to my family, and always gave in to her; but now I have somebody to stand by me," added Susan, fanning still more violently, and with a sound in her voice which betrayed a possibility of tears—"now I have somebody to stand by me—I tell you once for all, Nettie, I will not go on the 24th."

Nettie gazed at her sister in silence without attempting to say anything. Then she lifted her eyes inquiringly to the Australian, in his uneasy spectator position before the fire. She was not much discomposed, evidently, by that sudden assertion of will—possibly Nettie was used to it—but she looked curious and roused, and rather eager to know what was it now?

"I will not go on the 24th," cried Mrs Fred, with a hysterical toss of her head. "I will not be treated like a child, and told to get ready whenever Nettie pleases. She pretends it is all for our sake, but it is for the sake of having her own will, and because she has taken a sudden disgust at something. I asked you in, Mr Edward, because you are her friend, and because you are the children's uncle, and ought to know how they are provided for. Mr Chatham and I," said Susan, overcome by her feelings, and agitating the handkerchief violently, "have settled—to be—married first before we set out."

If a shell had fallen in the peaceful apartment, the effect could not have been more startling. The two who had been called in to receive that intimation, and who up to this moment had been standing together listening languidly enough, too much absorbed in the matter between themselves to be very deeply concerned about anything Mrs Fred could say or do, fell suddenly apart with the wildest amazement in their looks. "Susan, you are mad!"

cried Nettie, gazing aghast at her sister, with an air of mingled astonishment and incredulity. The doctor, too much excited to receive with ordinary decorum information so important, made a sudden step up to the big embarrassed Australian, who stood before the fire gazing into vacancy, and looking the very embodiment of conscious awkwardness. Dr Rider stretched out both his hands and grasped the gigantic fist of the Bushman with an effusion which took that worthy altogether by surprise. "My dear fellow, I wish you joy—I wish you joy. Anything I can be of use to you in, command me!" cried the doctor, with a suppressed shout of half-incredulous triumph. Then he returned restlessly towards Nettie—they all turned to her with instinctive curiosity. Never in all her troubles had Nettie been so pale; she looked in her sister's face with a kind of despair.

"Is this *true*, Susan?" she said, with a sorrowful wonder as different as possible from the doctor's joyful surprise—"not something said to vex us—really true? And this has been going on, and I knew nothing of it; and all this time you have been urging me to go back to the colony—*me*—as if you had no other thoughts. If you had made up your mind to this, what was the use of driving me desperate?" cried Nettie, in a sudden outburst of that incomprehension which aches in generous hearts. Then she stopped suddenly and looked from her sister, uttering suppressed sobs, and hiding her face in her handkerchief on the sofa, to the Australian before the fire. "What is the good of talking?" said Nettie, with a certain indignant impatient indulgence, coming to an abrupt conclusion. Nobody knew so well as she did how utterly useless it was to remonstrate or complain. She dropt into the nearest chair, and began with hasty tremulous hands to smooth down the cuffs of her black sleeves. In the bitterness of the moment it was not the sudden deliverance, but the heartlessness and domestic treachery that struck Nettie. She, the champion and defender of this helpless family for years— who had given them bread, and served it to them with her own cheerful unwearied hands—who had protected as well as

144

provided for them in her dauntless innocence and youth. When she was thus cast off on the brink of the costliest sacrifice of all, it was not the delightful sensation of freedom which occurred to Nettie. She fell back with a silent pang of injury swelling in her heart, and, all tremulous and hasty, gave her agitated attention to the simple act of smoothing down her sleeves—a simple but symbolical act, which conveyed a world of meaning to the mind of the doctor as he stood watching her. The work she had meant to do was over. Nettie's occupation was gone. With the next act of the domestic drama she had nothing to do. For the first time in her life utterly vanquished, with silent promptitude she abdicated on the instant. She seemed unable to strike a blow for the leadership thus snatched from her hands. With proud surprise and magnanimity she withdrew, forbearing even the useless reproaches of which she had impatiently asked, "What was the good?" Never abdicated emperor laid aside his robes with more ominous significance, than Nettie, with fingers trembling between haste and agitation, smoothed down round her shapely wrists those turned-up sleeves.

The doctor's better genius saved him from driving the indignant Titania desperate at that critical moment by any ill-advised rejoicings; and the sight of Nettie's agitation so far calmed Dr Rider that he made the most sober and decorous congratulations to the sister-in-law, whom for the first time he felt grateful to. Perhaps, had he been less absorbed in his own affairs, he could scarcely have failed to remember how, not yet a year ago, the shabby form of Fred lay on that same sofa from which Susan had announced her new prospects; but in this unexampled revolution of affairs no thought of Fred disturbed his brother, whose mind was thoroughly occupied with the sudden tumult of his own hopes. "Oh yes, I hope I shall be happy at last. After all my troubles, I have to look to myself, Mr Edward; and your poor brother would have been the last to blame me," sobbed Mrs Fred, with involuntary self-vindication. Then followed a pause. The change was too sudden and extraordinary, and involved results too deeply important to every individual present, to make words possible. Mrs Fred, with her face buried in her handkerchief, and Nettie, her whole frame thrilling with mortification and failure, tremulously trying to button her sleeves, and bestowing her whole mind upon that operation, were discouraging interlocutors; and after the doctor and the Bushman had shaken hands, their powers of communication were exhausted. The silence was at length broken by the Australian, who, clearing his voice between every three words, delivered his embarrassed sentiments as follows:—

"I trust, Miss Nettie, you'll not think you've been unfairly dealt by, or that any change is necessary so far as you are concerned. Of course," said Mr Chatham, growing red, and plucking at his beard, "neither your sister nor I—found out—till quite lately— how things were going to be; and as for you making any change in consequence, or thinking we could be anything but glad to have you with us——"

Here the alarming countenance of Nettie, who had left off buttoning her sleeves, brought her new relation to a sudden stop. Under the blaze of her inquiring eyes the Bushman could go no farther. He looked at Susan for assistance, but Susan was still absorbed in her handkerchief; and while he paused for expression, the little abdicated monarch took up the broken thread.

"Thank you," said Nettie, rising suddenly; "I knew you were honest. It is very good of you, too, to be glad to have me with you. You don't know any better. I'm abdicated, Mr Chatham; but because it's rather startling to have one's business taken out of one's hands like this, it will be very kind of everybody not to say anything more to-night. I don't quite understand it all just at this moment. Good-night, Dr Edward. We can talk to-morrow, please; not to-night. You surely understand me, don't you? When one's life is changed all in a moment, one does not exactly see where one is standing just at once. Good-night. I mean what I say," she continued, holding her head high with restrained excitement, and trying to conceal the nervous agitation which possessed her as the doctor hastened before her to open the door. "Don't come after me, please; don't say anything; I cannot bear any more to-night."

"But to-morrow," said the doctor, holding fast the trembling hand. Nettie was too much overstrained and excited to speak more. A single sudden sob burst from her as she drew her hand out of his, and disappeared like a flying sprite. The doctor saw the heaving of her breast, the height of self-restraint which could go no further. He went back into the parlour like a true lover, and spied no more upon Nettie's hour of weakness. Without her, it looked a vulgar scene enough in that little sitting-room, from which the smoke of Fred's pipe had never fairly disappeared, and where Fred himself had lain in dismal state. Dr Rider said a hasty good-night to Fred's successor, and went off hurriedly into the changed world which surrounded that unconscious cottage. Though the frost had not relaxed, and the air breathed no balm, no sudden leap from December to June could have changed the atmosphere so entirely to the excited wayfarer who traced back the joyful path towards the lights of Carlingford twinkling brilliant through the Christmas frost. As he paused to look back upon that house which now contained all his hopes, a sudden shadow appeared at a lighted window, looking out. Nettie could not see the owner of the footsteps which moved her to that sudden involuntary expression of what was in her thoughts, but he could see her standing full in the light, and the sight went to the doctor's heart. He took off his hat insanely in the darkness and waved his hand to her, though she could not see him; and, after the shadow had disappeared, continued to stand watching with tender folly if perhaps some indication of Nettie's presence might again reveal itself. He walked upon air as he went back, at last, cold but joyful, through the blank solitude of Grange Lane. Nothing could have come amiss to the doctor in that dawn of happiness. He could have found it in his heart to mount his drag again and drive ten miles in celestial patience at the call of any capricious invalid. He was half-disappointed to find no summons awaiting him when he went home—no outlet for the universal charity and loving-kindness that possessed him. Instead, he set his easy-chair tenderly by the side of the blazing fire, and, drawing another chair opposite, gazed with secret smiles at the visionary Nettie, who once had taken up her position there. Was it by prophetic instinct that the little colonial girl, whose first appearance so discomposed the doctor, had assumed that place? Dr Rider contemplated the empty chair with smiles that would have compromised his character for sanity with any uninstructed observer. When the mournful Mary disturbed his reverie by her noiseless and penitent entrance with the little supper which she meant at once for a peace-offering and compensation for the dinner lost, she carried down-stairs with her a vivid impression that somebody had left her master a fortune. Under such beatific circumstances closed the evening that had opened amid such clouds. Henceforth, so far as the doctor could read the future, no difficulties but those common to all wooers beset the course of his true love.

CHAPTER XVII.

When the red gleams of the early sunshine shone into that window from which Nettie had looked out last night, the wintry light came in with agitating revelations not simply upon another morning, but upon a new world. As usual, Nettie's thoughts were expressed in things tangible. She had risen from her sleepless bed while it was still almost dark, and to look at her now, a stranger might have supposed her to be proceeding with her last night's work with the constancy of a monomaniac. Little Freddy sat up in his crib rubbing his eyes and marvelling what Nettie could be about, as indeed anybody might have marvelled. With all those boxes and drawers about, and heaps of personal belongings, what was she going to do? She could not have answered the question without pain; but had you waited long enough, Nettie's object would have been apparent. Not entirely free of that air of agitated haste—not recovered from the excitement of this discovery, she was relieving her restless activity by a significant rearrangement of all the possessions of the family. She was separating with rapid fingers those stores which had hitherto lain lovingly together common property. For the first time for years Nettie had set herself to discriminate what belonged to herself from the general store; and, perhaps by way of softening that disjunction, was separating into harmonious order the little wardrobes which were no longer to be under her charge. Freddy opened his eyes to see all his own special belongings, articles which he recognised with all the tenacious proprietorship of childhood, going into one little box by themselves in dreadful isolation. The child did not know what horrible sentence might have been passed upon him while he slept. He gazed at those swift inexorable fingers with the gradual sob rising in his poor

149

little breast. That silent tempest heaved and rose as he saw all the well-known items following each other; and when his last new acquisition, the latest addition to his wardrobe, lay solemnly smoothed down upon the top, Freddy's patience could bear no more. Bursting into a long howl of affliction, he called aloud upon Nettie to explain that mystery. Was he going to be sent away? Was some mysterious executioner, black man, or other horrid vision of fate, coming for the victim? Freddy's appeal roused from her work the abdicated family sovereign. "If I'm to be sent away, I shan't go!" cried Freddy. "I'll run off and come back again. I shan't go anywhere unless you go, Nettie. I'll hold on so fast, you can't put me away; and, oh, I'll be good!—I'll be so good!" Nettie, who was not much given to caresses, came up and put sudden arms round her special nursling. She laid her cheek to his, with a little outbreak of natural emotion. "It is I who am to be sent away!" cried Nettie, yielding for a moment to the natural bitterness. Then she bethought herself of certain thoughts of comfort which had not failed to interject themselves into her heart, and withdrew with a little precipitation, alarmed by the inconsistency—the insincerity of her feelings. "Get up, Freddy; you are not going away, except home to the colony, where you want to go," she said. "Be good, all the same; for you know you must not trouble mamma. And make haste, and don't be always calling for Nettie. Don't you know you must do without Nettie some time? Jump up, and be a man."

"When I am a man, I shan't want you," said Freddy, getting up with reluctance; "but I can't be a man now. And what am I to do with the buttons if you won't help me? I shall not have buttons like those when I am a man."

It was not in human nature to refrain from giving the little savage an admonitory shake. "That is all I am good for—nothing but buttons!" said Nettie, with whimsical mortification. When they went down to breakfast, she sent the child before her, and came last instead of first, waiting till they were all assembled. Mrs Fred watched her advent with apprehensive eyes. Thinking it over after her first triumph, it occurred to Mrs Fred that the loss of Nettie would make a serious difference to her own comfort. Who was to take charge of the children, and conduct those vulgar affairs for which Susan's feelings disqualified her? She did her best to decipher the pale face which appeared over the breakfast cups and saucers opposite. What did Nettie mean to do? Susan revolved the question in considerable panic, seeing but too clearly that the firm little hand no longer trembled, and that Nettie was absorbed by her own thoughts—thoughts with which her present companions had but little to do. Mrs Fred essayed another stroke.

"Perhaps I was hasty, Nettie, last night; but Richard, you know, poor fellow," said Susan, "was not to be put off. It won't make any difference between you and me, Nettie dear? We have always been so united, whatever has happened; and the children are so fond of you; and as for me," said Mrs Fred, putting back the strings of her cap, and pressing her handkerchief upon her eyes, "with my health, and after all I have gone through, how I could ever exist without you, I can't tell; and Richard will be so pleased——"

"I don't want to hear anything about Richard, please," said Nettie—"not so far as I am concerned. I should have taken you out, and taken care of you, had you chosen me; but you can't have two people, you know. One is enough for anybody. Never mind what we are talking about, Freddy. It is only your buttons— nothing else. As long as you were my business, I should have scorned to complain," said Nettie, with a little quiver of her lip. "Nothing would have made me forsake you, or leave you to yourself; but now you are somebody else's business; and to speak of it making no difference, and Richard being pleased, and so forth, as if I had nothing else to do in the world, and wanted to go back to the colony! It is simply not my business any longer," cried Nettie, rising impatiently from her chair—"that is all that can be said. But I shan't desert you till I deliver you over to my successor, Susan—don't fear."

151

"Then you don't feel any love for us, Nettie! It was only because you could not help it. Children, Nettie is going to leave us," said Mrs Fred, in a lamentable voice.

"Then who is to be instead of Nettie? Oh, look here—I know—it's Chatham," said the little girl.

"I hate Chatham," said Freddy, with a little shriek. "I shall go where Nettie goes—all my things are in my box. Nettie is going to take me; she loves me best of you all. I'll kick Chatham if he touches me."

"Why can't some one tell Nettie she's to go too?" said the eldest boy. "She's most good of all. What does Nettie want to go away for? But I don't mind; for we have to do what Nettie tells us, and nobody cares for Chatham," cried the sweet child, making a triumphant somersault out of his chair. Nettie stood looking on, without attempting to stop the tumult which arose. She left them with their mother, after a few minutes, and went out to breathe the outside air, where at least there was quiet and freedom. To think as she went out into the red morning sunshine that her old life was over, made Nettie's head swim with bewildering giddiness. She went up softly, like a creature in a dream, past St Roque's, where already the Christmas decorators had begun their pretty work—that work which, several ages ago, being yesterday, Nettie had taken the children in to see. Of all things that had happened between that moment and this, perhaps the impulse of escaping out into the open air without anything to do, was one of the most miraculous. Insensibly Nettie's footsteps quickened as she became aware of that extraordinary fact. The hour, the temperature, the customs of her life, were equally against such an indulgence. It was a comfort to recollect that, though everything else in the universe was altered, the family must still have some dinner, and that it was as easy to think while walking to the butcher's as while idling and doing nothing. She went up, accordingly, towards Grange Lane, in a kind of wistful solitude, drifted apart from her former life, and not yet definitely attached to any other, feeling as though the few passengers she met must perceive in her face that her whole fortune was changed. It was hard for Nettie to realise that she could do absolutely nothing at this moment, and still harder for her to think that her fate lay undecided in Edward Rider's hands. Though she had not a doubt of him, yet the mere fact that it was he who must take the first step was somewhat galling to the pride and temper of the little autocrat. Before she had reached the butcher, or even come near enough to recognise Lucy Wodehouse, where she stood at the garden gate, setting out for St Roque's, Nettie heard the headlong wheels of something approaching which had not yet come in sight. She wound herself up in a kind of nervous desperation for the encounter that was coming. No need to warn her who it was. Nobody but the doctor flying upon wings of haste and love could drive in that break-neck fashion down the respectable streets of Carlingford. Here he came sweeping round that corner at the Blue Boar, where Nettie herself had once mounted the drag, and plunged down Grange Lane in a maze of speed which confused horse, vehicle, and driver in one indistinct gleaming circle to the excited eyes of the spectator, who forced herself to go on, facing them with an exertion of all her powers, and strenuous resistance of the impulse to turn and escape. Why should Nettie escape?—it must be decided one way or other. She held on dimly with rapid trembling steps. To her own agitated mind, Nettie, herself, left adrift and companionless, seemed the suitor. The only remnants of her natural force that remained to her united in the one resolution not to run away.

It was well for the doctor that his little groom had the eyes and activity of a monkey, and knew the exact moment at which to dart forward and catch the reins which his master flung at him, almost without pausing in his perilous career. The doctor made a leap out of the drag, which was more like that of a mad adventurer than a man whose business it was to keep other people's limbs in due repair. Before Nettie was aware that he had stopped, he was by her side.

"Dr Edward," she exclaimed, breathlessly, "hear me first! Now

I am left unrestrained, but I am not without resources. Don't think you are bound in honour to say anything over again. What may have gone before I forget now. I will not hold you to your word. You are not to have pity upon me!" cried Nettie, not well aware what she was saying. The doctor drew her arm into his; found out, sorely against her will, that she was trembling, and held her fast, not without a sympathetic tremor in the arm on which she was constrained to lean.

"But I hold you to yours!" said the doctor; "there has not been any obstacle between us for months but this; and now it is gone, do you think I will forget what you have said, Nettie? You told me it was impossible once——"

"And you did not contradict me, Dr Edward," said the wilful creature, withdrawing her hand from his arm. "I can walk very well by myself, thank you. You did not contradict me! You were content to submit to what could not be helped. And so am I. An obstacle which is only removed by Richard Chatham," said Nettie, with female cruelty, turning her eyes full and suddenly upon her unhappy lover, "does not count for much. I do not hold you to anything. We are both free."

What dismayed answer the doctor might have made to this heartless speech can never be known. He was so entirely taken aback that he paused, clearing his throat with but one amazed exclamation of her name; but before his astonishment and indignation had shaped itself into words, their interview was interrupted. An irregular patter of hasty little steps, and outcries of a childish voice behind, had not caught the attention of either in that moment of excitement; but just as Nettie delivered this cruel outbreak of feminine pride and self-assertion, the little pursuing figure made up to them, and plunged at her dress. Freddy, in primitive unconcern for anybody but himself, rushed head-foremost between these two at the critical instant. He made a clutch at Nettie with one hand, and with all the force of the other thrust away the astonished doctor. Freddy's errand was of life or death.

"I shan't go with any one but Nettie," cried the child, clinging to her dress. "I hate Chatham and everybody. I will jump into the sea and swim back again. I will never, never leave go of her, if you should cut my hands off. Nettie! Nettie!—take me with you. Let me go where you are going! I will never be naughty any more! I will never, never go away till Nettie goes! I love Nettie best! Go away, all of you!" cried Freddy, in desperation, pushing off the doctor with hands and feet alike. "I will stay with Nettie. Nobody loves Nettie but me."

Nettie had no power left to resist this new assault. She dropped down on one knee beside the child, and clasped him to her in a passion of restrained tears and sobbing. The emotion which her pride would not permit her to show before, the gathering agitation of the whole morning broke forth at this irresistible touch. She held Freddy close and supported herself by him, leaning all her troubled heart and trembling frame upon the little figure which clung to her bewildered, suddenly growing silent and afraid in that passionate grasp. Freddy spoke no more, but turned his frightened eyes upon the doctor, trembling with the great throbs of Nettie's breast. In the early wintry sunshine, on the quiet rural highroad, that climax of the gathering emotion of years befell Nettie. She could exercise no further self-control. She could only hide her face, that no one might see, and close her quivering lips tight that no one might hear the bursting forth of her heart. No one was there either to hear or see—nobody but Edward Rider, who stood bending with sorrowful tenderness over the wilful fairy creature, whose words of defiance had scarcely died from her lips. It was Freddy, and not the doctor, who had vanquished Nettie; but the insulted lover came in for his revenge. Dr Rider raised her up quietly, asking no leave, and lifted her into the drag, where Nettie had been before, and where Freddy, elated and joyful, took his place beside the groom, convinced that he was to go now with the only true guardian his little life had known. The doctor drove down that familiar road as slowly as he had dashed furiously up to it. He took quiet possession of the agitated trembling creature who had carried her empire over herself too far. At last Nettie had broken down; and now he had it all his own way.

When they came to the cottage, Mrs Fred, whom excitement had raised to a troublesome activity, came eagerly out to the door to see what had happened; and the two children, who, emancipated from all control, were sliding down the banisters of the stair, one after the other, in wild glee and recklessness, paused in their dangerous amusement to watch the new arrival. "Oh! look here; Nettie's crying!" said one to the other, with calm observation. The words brought Nettie to herself.

"I am not crying now," she said, waking into sudden strength. "Do you want to get them killed before they go away, all you people? Susan, go in, and never mind. I was not—not quite well out of doors; but I don't mean to suffer this, you know, as long as I am beside them. Dr Edward, come in. I have something to say to you. We have nowhere to speak to each other but here," said Nettie, pausing in the little hall, from which that childish tumult had died away in sudden awe of her presence; "but we have spoken to each other here before now. I did not mean to vex you then—at least, I did mean to vex you, but nothing more." Here she paused with a sob, the echo of her past trouble breaking upon her words, as happened from time to time, like the passion of a child; then burst forth again a moment after in a sudden question. "Will you let me have Freddy?" she cried, surrendering at discretion, and looking eagerly up in the doctor's face; "if they will leave him, may I keep him with me?"

It is unnecessary to record the doctor's answer. He would have swallowed not Fred only, but Mrs Fred and the entire family, had that gulp been needful to satisfy Nettie, but was not sufficiently blinded to his own interests to grant this except under certain conditions satisfactory to himself. When the doctor mounted the drag again he drove away into Elysium, with a smiling Cupid behind him, instead of the little groom who had been his unconscious master's confidant so long, and had watched the fluctuations of his wooing with such lively curiosity. Those patients who had paid for Dr Rider's disappointments in many a violent prescription, got compensation to-day in honeyed draughts and hopeful prognostications. Wherever the doctor went he saw a vision of that little drooping head, reposing, after all the agitation of the morning, in the silence and rest he had enjoined, with brilliant eyes, half-veiled, shining with thoughts in which he had the greatest share; and, with that picture before his eyes, went flashing along the wintry road with secret smiles, and carried hope wherever he went. Of course it was the merest fallacy, so far as Nettie's immediate occupation was concerned. That restless little woman had twenty times too much to do to think of rest—more to do than ever in all the suddenly-changed preparations which fell upon her busy hands. But the doctor kept his imagination all the same, and pleased himself with thoughts of her reposing in a visionary tranquillity, which, wherever it was to be found, certainly did not exist in St Roque's Cottage, in that sudden tumult of new events and hopes.

CHAPTER XVIII.

"I always thought there was good in him by his looks," said Miss Wodehouse, standing in the porch of St Roque's, after the wedding-party had gone away. "To think he should have come in such a sweet way and married Mrs Fred! just what we all were wishing for, if we could have ventured to think it possible. Indeed, I should have liked to have given Mr Chatham a little present, just to mark my sense of his goodness. Poor man! I wonder if he repents——"

"It is to be hoped not yet," said Lucy, hurrying her sister away before Mr Wentworth could come out and join them; for affairs were seriously compromised between the perpetual curate and the object of his affections; and Lucy exhibited a certain acerbity under the circumstances which somewhat amazed the tender-hearted old maid.

"When people do repent, my belief is that they do it directly," said Miss Wodehouse. "I daresay he can see what she is already, poor man; and I hope, Lucy, it won't drive him into bad ways. As for Nettie, I am not at all afraid about her. Even if they should happen to quarrel, you know, things will always come right. I am glad they were not married both at the same time. Nettie has such sense! and of course, though it was the very best thing that could happen, and a great relief to everybody concerned, to be sure, one could not help being disgusted with that woman. And it is such a comfort they're going away. Nettie says——"

"Don't you think you could walk a little quicker? there is somebody in Grove Street that I have to see," said Lucy, not so much interested as her sister; "and papa will be home at one to lunch."

"Then I shall go on, dear, if you have no objection, and ask when the doctor and Nettie are coming home," said Miss Wodehouse, "and take poor little Freddy the cakes I promised him. Poor child! to have his mother go off and marry and leave him. Never mind me, Lucy, dear; I do not walk so quickly as you do, and besides I have to go home first for the cakes."

So saying the sisters separated; and Miss Wodehouse took her gentle way to the doctor's house, where everything had been brightened up, and where Freddy waited the return of his chosen guardians. It was still the new quarter of Carlingford, a region of half-built streets, vulgar new roads, and heaps of desolate brick and mortar. If the doctor had ever hoped to succeed Dr Marjoribanks in his bowery retirement in Grange Lane, that hope nowadays had receded into the darkest distance. The little surgery round the corner still shed twinkles of red and blue light across that desolate triangle of unbuilt ground upon the other corner houses where dwelt people unknown to society in Carlingford, and still Dr Rider consented to call himself M.R.C.S., and cultivate the patients who were afraid of a physician. Miss Wodehouse went in at the invitation of Mary to see the little drawing-room which the master of the house had provided for his wife. It had been only an unfurnished room in Dr Rider's bachelor days, and looked out upon nothing better than these same new streets—the vulgar suburb which Carlingford disowned. Miss Wodehouse lingered at the window with a little sigh over the perversity of circumstances. If Miss Marjoribanks had only been Nettie, or Nettie Miss Marjoribanks! If not only love and happiness, but the old doctor's practice and savings, could but have been brought to heap up the measure of the young doctor's good-fortune! What a pity that one cannot have everything! The friendly visitor said so with a real sigh as she went down-stairs after her inspection. If the young people had but been settling in Grange Lane, in good society, and with Dr Marjoribanks's practice, this marriage would have been perfection indeed!

But when the doctor brought Nettie home, and set her in that easy-chair which her image had possessed so long, he saw few drawbacks at that moment to the felicity of his lot. If there was one particular in which his sky threatened clouds, it was not the want of Dr Marjoribanks's practice, but the presence of that little interloper, whom the doctor in his heart was apt to call by uncomplimentary names, and did not regard with unmixed favour. But when Susan and her Australian were fairly gone, and all fear of any invasion of the other imps—which Dr Rider inly dreaded up to the last moment—was over, Freddy grew more and more tolerable. Where Fred once lay and dozed, and filled the doctor's house with heavy fumes and discreditable gossip, a burden on his brother's reluctant hospitality, little Freddy now obliterated that dismal memory with prayers and slumbers of childhood; and where the discontented doctor had grumbled many a night and day over that bare habitation of his, which was a house, and not a home, Nettie diffused herself till the familiar happiness became so much a part of his belongings that the doctor learned to grumble once more at the womanish accessories which he had once missed so bitterly. And the little wayward heroine who, by dint of hard labour and sacrifice, had triumphantly had her own way in St Roque's Cottage, loved her own way still in the new house, and had it as often as was good for her. But so far as this narrator knows, nothing calling for special record has since appeared in the history of the doctor's family, thus reorganised under happier auspices, and discharging its duties, social and otherwise, though not exactly in society, to the satisfaction and approval of the observant population of Carlingford.

THE END.